THE TELL TALE HEART PIN

A LAKE HOPE MYSTERY

LEAH R CUTTER

KNOTTED ROAD PRESS

The Tell Tale Heart Pin
A Lake Hope Mystery
Copyright © 2021 Leah Cutter

Published by Knotted Road Press
www.KnottedRoadPress.com

ISBN: 978-1-64470-227-7

Cover Art:
ID 149501307 © Porntep Lueangon | Dreamstime.com

ID 65654416 © Stephen Dumayne | Dreamstime.com

Cover and interior design copyright © 2021 Knotted Road Press
http://www.KnottedRoadPress.com

Reviews
It's true. Reviews help me sell more books. If you've enjoyed this story, please consider leaving a review of it on your favorite site.

Come someplace new…
Are you a traveler? Do you enjoy exploring strange new worlds, new cultures, new people?

Journey into the various lands envisioned by Leah Cutter.

Sign up for my newsletter and I'll start you on your travels with a free copy of my book, *The Island Sampler*.

I will never spam you or use your email for nefarious purposes. You can also unsubscribe at any time.

http://www.LeahCutter.com/newsletter/

ALSO BY LEAH R CUTTER

Forgotten Gods

A Wind Blown Torment

A Stone Strewn Clash

A Sea Washed Victory

Tanish Empire Trilogy

The Glass Magician

The Desert Heart

The Ghost Dog

The Cassie Stories

Poisoned Pearls

Tainted Waters

Spoiled Harvest

Bloodied Ice

The Witch's Progress

Circle of Air

Circle of Water

Circle of Fire

Circle of Earth

Seattle Trolls

The Changeling Troll

The Princess Troll

The Fairy-Bridge Troll

The Troll-Demon War

The Troll-Human War

The Troll-Troll War

The Shadow Wars Trilogy

The Raven and the Dancing Tiger

The Guardian Hound

War Among the Crocodiles

The Clockwork Fairy Kingdom

The Clockwork Fairy Kingdom

The Maker, the Teacher, and the Monster

The Dwarven Wars

The Chronicles of Franklin

Franklin Versus The Popcorn Thief

Franklin Versus The Soul Thief

Franklin Versus The Child Thief

Huli Intergalactic - Science/Space Fantasy

Origins

The Strawberry Girl

1

"Well, it's about time," a nasty, nasal voice greeted the bus driver's announcement that they'd arrived at Heart Vineyards, the last stop of their tour.

Lydia Marsh pressed her lips together firmly so she wouldn't make some snide remark about how happy she'd be to get out of the bus and away from Richard "Ricky" Hollingsworth. He was a guest staying at her B&B, though he was never coming back as far as she was concerned.

She'd been initially pleased that a vaguely famous musician was being put up at her B&B. She didn't learn until later that Ricky had worn out his welcome at every other establishment in town.

He was there for a week, playing his guitar down at *The Cove* every night. Thirty years ago he'd had a single hit and had been milking it ever since.

Ricky stomped off the mini-bus, shoving other people aside impatiently. He wore a white, long-sleeved shirt with a black string tie, black hat, and black boots. Supposedly a renegade cowboy, complete with greasy long hair. Lydia didn't see the appeal.

Or as her dear gay uncles, Ed and Alan, had said once, "All hat, no cattle."

A hand touched hers, and Lydia glanced over at Ellis Avery, her long-distance boyfriend for the last year. He smiled at her, his blue eyes warm. He wore a gray T-shirt that showed off his very nice muscular shoulders and chest. "It's probably a good thing that you insisted I leave my gun back at the B&B. Otherwise, I might have had to shoot that asshole."

Lydia snorted. "Or I would have."

She appreciated that Ellis was trying to make light of one of the constant sore spots between them. As Ellis was a police detective from the city of Yakima, he always felt better armed.

Lydia didn't like it when Ellis was carrying. When Ellis was in "boyfriend" mode he was fun, charming, sexy, and Lydia enjoyed his company very much.

However, when he was armed, he was much more likely to drop into "cop" mode, when he became very cold, maintaining a three-foot-glass barrier that wasn't much fun to be around.

Lydia tried to accept that it was just part of Ellis, but she wasn't always successful.

They waited at the back of the mini-bus for the other passengers to depart. Since Lydia ran a B&B in the nearby town of Lake Hope, along with a restaurant playfully called *Nip & Bud*, she tried to get out and do some of the touristy things in the area. This way, she'd have first-hand experience of them to tell her guests about. Particularly now that she had someone to go try things with.

The Heart Vineyards and Winery was relatively new, just opening up that summer. They'd bought out the family who'd owned the property previously. Lydia was looking forward to trying their wines. If she liked any of them, she might ask if they'd consider doing a wine tasting back at the *Nip & Bud* sometime.

Warm August air engulfed them as they stepped out of the air conditionedvehicle, melting Lydia's bones in a good way. A few white clouds dotted the clear blue skies, lifting her spirits. Beyond the brightly painted, red buildings, rows of grapes grew, lush and flourishing.

While Lake Hope was barely a town, much less a city, Lydia still enjoyed getting out into the countryside on a regular basis. The quiet would get to her after a while, but for now, it was lovely, the wide open area, the smell of green growing things, the sun warming her head.

Lydia was dressed for the mid-August weather in central Washington, wearing light-blue denim shorts, sandals, and a cream-colored top that fit comfortably across her wide shoulders and chest. Her hair was tied in a tight braid, hanging down to the middle of her back. She stretched her arms over her head, noticed that Ellis was eyeing her, and bent over with a shimmy, showing off her butt.

Lydia was tall, five-eleven, and all leg. She knew how to show that off for her beau.

When she stood back up, Ellis came up behind her, wrapping his arms around her and kissing her on the neck. Lydia put her arms up and tousled the brown hair that had a few more gray strands in it since when she'd first met him a year or so ago.

They exchanged a sweet kiss, then walked up to join the others. The building was a converted barn, painted bright red with white trim, two-stories high with a steeply pitched roof. The group went through a simple door next to the large barn door.

The interior didn't look like a barn at all, but instead, like a high-end display room. The loft had been removed, making the space seem huge. Polished concrete made up the floor, and discreet orangish lights kept the area dim. Glass cabinets lined the walls, showing various bottles of wine, all with the Heart label.

About ten feet inside the door, a long counter ran all the way across the building A plexiglass barrier ran across the top of it. Lydia, Ellis, and the others on the tour stood on their side of the counter while the woman giving the tour stood on the other.

At least they didn't have to wear masks anymore! After a year and a half of awfulness, most everything was back to normal.

Or a new normal, at any rate.

The woman leading the tour was wearing a mask, but, as she explained, that was because she was closer to the vats where they made the wine. Huge stainless steel barrels filled the rest of the barn. They were each ten feet in diameter according to Nancy, who was leading the tour. The barrels were built in a clever honeycomb configuration, and they used rolling ladders to access every barrel.

Though the Heart family had bought this property

only a year ago, they'd already been making wine at a different location for years. They used grapes from not only this farm but several others in the region, though they were looking forward to primarily using grapes from their own property now.

It was an interesting tour, and Nancy was a charming speaker. If she'd come and do the wine tastings at the B&B, Lydia would be pleased.

It occurred to her about midway through that Ricky wasn't there to spoil their enjoyment. He hadn't actually done the tour at the last vineyard either, but had gone straight to the tasting room. Maybe that was where he was now.

Fortunately, no one would serve him if he appeared drunk, so that had moderated his behavior slightly.

After the tour, Lydia and Ellis followed behind the others from the barn to the tasting room.

While the wine making facilities had been shiny and new, the tasting room still needed to be updated. Old-fashioned frescos of grapes hanging from vines decorated the walls between the tops of the windows and the ceiling. The windows looked out over a pretty garden filled with dahlias, cone flowers, and sunflowers. Walls had been painted to look "rustic," as though they were made out of stucco peeling off brick. Instead of being charming, it just looked shabby. The floor was nice, though, covered in long pieces of tile that looked like hardwood.

Only a few scuffed-up tables were scattered across the open area. Lydia would bet that only half as many chairs were placed in front of the bar as there had once been.

Lydia had made similar changes to the *Nip and Bud*,

her restaurant attached to the B&B. She'd removed tables and opened up the seating area to comply with the new government requirements regarding restaurant seating. Then she'd come to realize that she really liked the new table arrangement. It gave the restaurant a much more open feeling.

Similarly, too many tables or chairs in the tasting room would have detracted from its charm, she was sure. The gaps were probably for ambience rather than reduced demand.

She considered pointing this out to Ellis, but didn't.

Just as she didn't appreciate Ellis pointing out to her all the exits in a room and the general threat assessment of everyone in a place they were visiting, he didn't enjoy all the restaurant details that she thrived on.

One of the advantages of not driving themselves on a winery tour meant that Lydia didn't have to worry about how much she was drinking. A full flight of wine tasting —another six glasses—wouldn't necessarily bother her.

But this was the third vineyard that day, and she might have been slightly tipsy.

At least that was what she blamed her roaming eye on.

The man behind the counter of the wine-tasting room was certainly handsome. He was rugged, like Ellis, which appeared to be her type now. He had copper colored hair that swept back from his broad forehead in waves, searing blue eyes, and thin sensuous lips. He wore a long-sleeved green shirt that really set off his pale coloring and freckles.

Ellis noticed her wandering eye. "Good thing I'm not the jealous type," he said dryly.

"Sorry," Lydia said. She reached across the table and

squeezed his hand. "You know window shopping doesn't really matter, right? As long as I always eat at home?"

Ellis snorted. "I hadn't heard that expression before, but you're right." He used their joined hands to pull her in for another sweet kiss.

By the time they'd finished trying all the different wines, Lydia was definitely feeling the alcohol. Her insides were warm and everything was slightly out of focus.

She'd have to sober up once they got back to the B&B. She had guests to greet that night, as Misty had been taking care of everything that day. Plus, it was Thursday night, and every room was going to be full through the weekend.

It wasn't until she and Ellis were walking back to the bus, carrying a box with six bottles of wine, that Lydia realized that Ricky hadn't been making a scene in this wine tasting room either.

Maybe he'd made good on his threat to hire a cab to take him back to the hotel?

Ellis went to the back of the bus with their wine while Lydia checked with Susan, the bus driver.

"Have you seen Ricky?" Lydia asked.

"Not since he left in a huff, no," Susan said. She reminded Lydia of Misty, as they were both short, stout, older Hispanic women. Possibly they were related, as Misty appeared to have cousins and other relations everywhere.

"So you didn't see a taxi come and pick him up?" Lydia said.

"No such luck," Susan said. "No one else came or left

while we've been here." "We could just leave without him," Susan suggested.

"Don't tempt me," Lydia said. Though she doubted that Ricky would bother leaving her a good review on any of the rental sites, she still didn't want to deliberately upset him.

After everyone else had made it onto the bus with their purchases, Lydia stood up and asked, "Has anyone seen Ricky?"

"No," came the consensus.

She might have only been imagining the comment of, "Good riddance."

"I'm going to see if I can find him," she announced, smiling at the groans she received in response. "I won't take too long," she promised.

Lydia walked back out into the August heat. She honestly wasn't going to spend much time looking for her errant guest. It was far too hot and she had things to do back at the B&B.

Besides, Ricky was a grown man with a cell phone and credit cards. He could get himself back to the B&B if necessary.

Lydia walked to the barn where they made the wine and poked her head inside. The lights had been dimmed further. She took a step inside. "Hello?" she called.

No one answered.

As she was walking toward the wine tasting room, she heard a commotion back behind the barn.

The young man from the wine tasting room came rushing around the end of the building. He ran straight to her, his blue eyes wide, his pale face even whiter, the freckles standing out across his nose and cheeks.

"You can't go back there," he stated, grabbing her forearms.

"What? What do you mean? What happened?"

"There's—there's a body back there!" The poor man shook his head and shivered. "Stabbed in the heart by one of our temperature gauges. With one of our heart stickers covering the gage."

Lydia shivered. She remembered seeing the thermometers as part of the tour. They were long, perhaps two to three feet, with a round gauge on the end and a very sharp, pointed end on the other.

"Who is it?" she asked, though she knew who it had to be.

"I don't know," the man said. "Someone with your tour. White shirt, black cowboy hat?"

Lydia nodded. "And black boots."

It had to be Ricky.

Everyone had wanted him dead. But who had actually gone ahead and done it?

2

_____

*L*ydia wasn't steaming angry when she finally made it back to the *Nip & Bud*. Just a little hot under the collar. She understood that Ellis considered it part of his job to stay with the body and work with the local police.

On the other hand, a murder, even of someone as deserving as Ricky, was disturbing, and she really wished she had a more normal boyfriend. Someone who would have held her hand or hugged her on the trip back to Lake Hope.

Lydia had texted Misty and told her to make sure that the door to Ricky's room was locked. She even went so far as to ask Misty to put some tape across the door with a "Do Not Enter" sign.

Ricky had been staying in the Cornflower rooms, on the second floor. All the rooms were named after edible flowers that Lydia used in the teas she served. The walls were the color of blue bachelor buttons, with matching comforter and pillows. Cornflower was one of the two large rooms on that floor that had its own *ensuite*, while the two smaller rooms on each floor shared a bathroom.

How long would it be before she could use that room again? How long would the police hold it? Lydia's mind instantly leapt to the worst possible scenario, that she'd be without that room for the rest of the year.

Which was nonsense. She shook her head. No, they'd only need it for a day, maybe two. As it was Thursday, and Ricky was supposed to be staying with her until Tuesday, they could have it until then. Then she needed to change it over for the next guests.

At least Ricky hadn't died at the B&B! That would have been awful. And the room really would have been off limits for weeks.

Misty had agreed to stay late to greet the first guests who arrived that afternoon. Lydia came walking in to find more guests waiting on the ground floor. She showed them their rooms, explaining the quirks of the heating and cooling, as well as their breakfast options.

Nip and Bud served breakfast and lunch, but not dinner. She'd been so supported by the community when everything had shut down and the tourists had stopping coming in the year before. She still had regulars among the locals who ordered sandwiches and salads to go on a daily or weekly basis.

When Lydia finished showing the last guests their room, she came back downstairs to see Misty waiting for her.

Lydia wanted to scold Misty for not going home, particularly after she'd covered for Lydia all afternoon while she went on the vineyard tour. However, Lydia was really glad to see her friend.

Misty had a way of making everyone around her feel better. It wasn't just the fact that she had a perpetual smile. Misty was happy with who she was, content, and that made everyone around her comfortable as well.

That night, she wore her coarse brown hair pulled back with a pretty blue headband, which matched her light-blue T-shirt. She was chatting in Spanish with someone on the phone, but made her excuses and hung up when she saw Lydia.

"Everyone settled?" Misty asked. Though they'd seen each other in passing when Lydia had finally returned from the wine tour, they hadn't really had a chance to talk.

"They are," Lydia said. "And now, I need a large glass of wine to help settle me."

Misty gave her a sharp look. "And where is that man of yours?"

"He's off playing cop," Lydia said. She hadn't meant to sound so sharp, but she couldn't help it. It had been a long day and she had no idea when Ellis would return.

Misty shook her head but didn't say anything. She so rarely ever said anything bad about anyone that Lydia was neither surprised nor hurt.

"I can stay with you until he gets back," Misty offered.

Lydia smile and shook her head. "Thank you. I appreciate the offer, but I'm okay."

Misty stubbornly walked forward and put her arms around Lydia, engulfing her in a tight, motherly hug.

Lydia found herself breathing a huge sigh of relief. She'd been a lot more tense than she'd realized. "Thank you," she told her friend, holding on for a few more moments, soaking up the comfort that Misty exuded, along with the faint scent of corn tortillas.

"Are you sure you don't need me to stay?" Misty said as she drew back.

"I'll be fine," Lydia assured her. "Now, go to your family! They need you as well."

Misty gave her a grin. "They know better than to question when Mama needs to work."

"But you don't always have to work, right?" Lydia teased. It was an old joke between them, how she never took a day off. However, over the past year, Lydia had taken a lot of time off.

"Exactly," Misty said, nodding solemnly. She turned away and was halfway across the room to the door before she turned back and said, "I will not speak ill of the dead. I just hope that Mr. Hollingsworth is happier now, than he was when he was with the living."

"I hope the same for him," Lydia said, nodding.

The man had been horrible, but possibly he'd been a charming boy. Or a good husband. She knew nothing of him, except that he'd complained about everything—the coffee was too bitter (it wasn't), the rolls she served weren't fresh (they'd come that morning from Patrice's bakery, so they certainly were), and even that the room smelled funny.

Lydia couldn't do anything about the latter, besides walk into the room and tell him that it smelled fine to her.

Though she would admit that there had been a floral scent in the room that had surprised her. She would have thought that Ricky would wear a masculine aftershave or something similar. The light, springy scent had been a surprise.

Or maybe he'd had a woman come up to visit him, despite the wedding ring he wore.

Lydia looked at her own empty fingers, then snorted at herself. Even if she were married, she probably wouldn't wear a ring. She was forever sticking her hands in gunk, cleaning. She tried to wear gloves, but frequently found herself out of patience or time.

She spent a moment looking out over the closed restaurant area of the *Nip and Bud*. Instead of the dozen tables that had been scattered haphazardly across the floor, there were now merely eight, though now they were of different sizes.

One of the smaller tables was in the far corner, next to the (currently unlit) fireplace with the white mantel. The other small table was close to the bay window, looking out on the sleepy Main Street of Lake Hope. The wall between them was covered in a chic, white-and-rose-colored graphic wallpaper. While Lydia loved the motif, she knew that she was going to have to change it up, possibly that winter during the off season. Maybe she could find that beautiful gold swirl design she'd seen in a recent home improvement magazine.

Scattered across the wall were floating shelves holding teapots, some modern, some antique. They really added to the ambiance of the restaurant, along with the original hard-wood floors that glowed golden in the sunlight.

To Lydia's right stood the counter where the altar to a modern god stood—the gleaming silver coffee urn. Behind the counter were built-in shelves, placed there by the building owners in the 1950s, back when it was a general store, before Lydia had remodeled it into a B&B. They held all the glassware, cloth napkins, plates, and silverware the restaurant needed.

Lydia let out a contented sigh. She loved this place so much. She'd put so much work into it. Last year had been admittedly rough. Luckily, she'd been able to weather the changes, in part with a loan from her parents.

Their original plan for the year had been to buy an RV and go explore the country. However, that hadn't happened. Instead, they'd loaned Lydia the money, and had stayed in town.

On the one hand, Lydia was grateful for their support. She was paying them back slowly. On the other hand, it meant that her mom had had too much time on her hands, and so had gotten into the last thing in the world that Lydia enjoyed, namely, politics.

That fall, her mom was running for the Judiciary Advisory Committee. Most of the members of the board were selected from other departments, such as the Department of Corrections or the Sheriff. However, there were three citizen members on the committee who were elected.

Her mom had the background to run for the office—for most of her adult life she'd worked as a legal secretary for the one honest lawyer in town.

But she was running against the incumbent, Alan Turflow, who was one of the crooked lawyers in town.

Even though her mom's chances didn't look good, Lydia still refused to put up political banners in her B&B. She'd alienate half of the town if she did that, and she needed the goodwill of the locals. Particularly given how they'd supported her this last year.

Lydia shook her head and made her way to her apartment, specially built at the back of the B&B.

Politics, taxes, and death.

All things sure to bring a girl down.

However, there would be good wine in her future. And maybe Ellis would arrive after too long. Both of those were sure to cheer her up.

3
_____

$\mathcal{L}$ ydia could practically see the anger rolling off Ellis in waves as he came into her apartment at the back of the B&B.

She sat curled up in the wingback chair, a glass of wine on the small table beside her, along with her ebook reader. The room was the perfect size for one, and a bit more crowded but still comfy with two. She didn't bother with a kitchen back here—when she wanted to fix herself something, she could just use the restaurant kitchen. She did have a small, apartment-sized fridge for her food and her wine.

"What is it?" Lydia asked as Ellis paced across the thick rug.

"My CO decided to not put me in charge of the case," Ellis grumbled. "He assigned it to Joe Blowhard instead."

"Joe Blowhard?" Lydia said. She couldn't help but smile at the name.

A look of horror crossed Ellis's face. "I shouldn't have said that out loud. I'm sorry. Detective Joseph Bloyer will be taking the case. You'll get a chance to meet him in the morning."

"I'm sure it'll be fine," Lydia said soothingly. "Can I get you something to eat? Some wine, perhaps?"

Ellis shook his head and collapsed on the purple micro-suede loveseat under the window, opposite to where Lydia sat. "Thanks," he said. "I'm going to need to drive back to Yakima in the morning."

"All right," Lydia said, trying to suppress her disappointment. Scheduling was always an issue between them. The police in Yakima were short-staffed, and Ellis was constantly working doubles and triples. While Lydia had had some time off the previous year, now, it was tourist season, and she wasn't going to be able to sneak in a whole day off until October.

They'd make it work. Though it would take effort on both their parts.

Ed and Alan had tried to give her as much relationship advice as they could. They were an old married couple, so they couldn't help much with a new relationship. They'd lived together for years under the fiction that they were just roommates, despite being in a one-room apartment. They'd been able to get married eventually and were happier for it.

They'd both told her about the work a partnership took, the constant adjusting and tweaking of the relationship. She'd taken their advice to heart, happy to do the work. She was never sure, though, if Ellis felt the same way.

While Ed and Alan had loved the pictures of Ellis that she'd sent them, they had, of course, disparaged his fashion sense. They even went so far as to claim that their cat Poe was more stylish.

Which was ridiculous. Poe was innately fashionable, with sleek black fur, huge green eyes, and a golden collar. No one could measure up to him.

"Want to go to bed? And cuddle?" Lydia asked after Ellis spent a bit more time just staring up at the ceiling. It was an awfully nice ceiling, made out of warm cedar wood boards. When Lydia had been building her apartment, she'd made every design decision based on whether the result would delight her or not. It wasn't good enough to just be pretty or functional. No, it had to be both, as well as delightful.

"Sorry, I'm still too worked up," Ellis said after a moment. "Maybe I should just drive back to Yakima now."

"Are you okay to drive?" Lydia asked, not surprised. She'd seen Ellis like this before.

Ellis took her question seriously, pausing to consider it for a while. "I am," he finally decided. He stood up and walked over to where she was still sitting. "Thank you for understanding," he said, giving her a good solid kiss.

Lydia felt something melt inside her as they kissed. Ellis was sometimes like a warm fireplace, comforting and homey.

But he didn't allow the kiss to grow deeper or hotter. With a sad smile, Ellis pulled away, then walked into the bedroom to pack his bag.

Lydia stayed where she was, knowing that Ellis was doing what was right for him.

Whether it was the right thing for her, or for them as a couple, she couldn't say.

After just a short while, Ellis came out, his bag in one hand. He'd found the box containing the mix of bottles from the various vineyards that Lydia had prepared for him and carried that in his other hand.

"I'm off," he said, coming over to give her a peck on the cheek. "I don't know when I'll be able to break free again."

Lydia nodded. She didn't know when her next break would be coming either. She'd been looking forward to having something of a weekend with her boyfriend.

"I'll call tomorrow," Ellis promised. He was mostly good about those sorts of things.

"I'm looking forward to it," Lydia said.

One last quick kiss, then Ellis left.

And Lydia was alone again. Or perhaps, as always.

4

$\mathcal{L}$unch rush Friday seemed particularly busy. Lydia felt as though she was walking her feet off as she went from the restaurant, back to the kitchen, then out again, carrying sandwiches, salads, soup and drinks, checking on her guests, bringing more coffee, returning with checks, and so on. It was a good thing she wore a light-weight blue blouse that morning, along with jean shorts. Her hair was pulled back into its usual ponytail, with plain bobby pins ensuring that the little short hairs around her face and ears didn't fly free.

Just as the rush was starting to clear, someone else came in the door. "I'll be right with you," Lydia called to the man standing there.

"Ma'am, I'd appreciate it if you'd see me now," the stranger said.

It took Lydia a moment to realize that this person screamed "cop."

He was dressed in an ill-fitting gray suit. She didn't want to even think about what Ed and Alan might say, how he needed a tailor to shorten the cuffs on the jacket, as well as the pants. The shirt was an off-white that did nothing for the man's florid complexion. His small, squinting eyes stared hard at her above pudgy cheeks, as if he'd already examined her and found her wanting. The mud brown tie just didn't match the outfit at all. Hopefully the stain on the side of it was from that morning, and not left over from the previous week. Or month.

"Ah. You must be Detective Bloyer," Lydia said, coming over and nodding at the man, her hands conveniently full of dishes at the moment so she didn't have to shake his hand. "The lunch rush is nearly over. Can I get you a cup of coffee or something?"

His thin lips pressed together as if he was trying to stop himself from yelling at her. He looked sourly around the restaurant before he said, "Don't you have any help?"

"Yes, but she's in the kitchen, making food," Lydia snapped. "I will be finished here as soon as is humanly possible," she promised him.

The detective gave her a sharp nod. "I'll wait. For a short while," he warned.

He walked away from her, into the gift shop located on the other side of the stairs. Lydia sold knickknacks there, such as beautiful tea sets and local honey in small hand-blown glass bottles. She also carried books, maps, hand-painted coasters, coffee mugs, and wine glasses. Some of the trinkets branded with *Nip and Bud* were made out of the gorgeous purple agate found locally.

Lydia let Misty know that the detective from Yakima had arrived, then tried to rush through her last few customers. Fate played against her, though, and it turned out that one had a dairy allergy that she hadn't bothered mentioning earlier, so her salad had needed to be swapped out, while a second demanded a new sandwich, one without tomatoes.

Finally, Lydia felt as though she could leave her customers and find the detective. He was paging through one of the books about local ghosts when she came up.

"My apologies for making you wait so long," Lydia said.

Detective Bloyer merely nodded. "I understand," he said, though it didn't sound as if he did. "Tell me, do you believe in ghosts?"

Lydia gave her standard answer, the one she used with her guests and other tourists. "I've never seen one, but Misty swears that the B&B is haunted."

"Misty Martinez? Your help?" the detective asked, finally putting the book away.

"My employee," Lydia emphasized.

"Yes, right," Detective Bloyer said, nodding. "And what about your other employee? Alice McGowen?"

"She doesn't believe in ghosts," Lydia said with a smile. "She thinks they're just stories." Alice was developmentally disabled, and primarily helped Lydia with the cleaning of the eight rooms, above. She'd been raised on a farm and was very strong. She also had a sweet nature and had been raised well by her parents to be unafraid to tell people what she really thought.

"So you don't think that the ghost of Richard Hollingsworth will come to haunt you?" the detective said.

Lydia shrugged her shoulders. "I don't see why he should. He wasn't killed here."

"No, he was killed at the Heart vineyard, on a tour that you arranged," Detective Bloyer said.

"I arrange a lot of tours for my guests," Lydia said defensively. Surely he wasn't accusing her of setting Ricky up?

"And what about your friend, Patrice Skahonish?" the detective said.

"What about her?" Lydia said, confused.

"Aren't you her best friend?" the detective countered. "She had a restraining order out against Mr. Hollingsworth."

"She did?" Lydia said, completely surprised. "I didn't know!"

The detective peered at her with his beady eyes. He finally nodded, appearing to believe her. "So you have no idea where she was yesterday while you were out on a wine tour with your boyfriend?"

"None," Lydia said. She hadn't texted Patrice or called her. Hell, she hadn't talked with her that day.

Surely the detective didn't think that Patrice was a suspect? Patrice wouldn't kill anybody, not unless her own life was in imminent danger.

But Lydia wasn't about to bring that up to the detective.

"I've closed off the room that Ricky was staying in," Lydia assured the detective when he didn't say anything more, but merely stared at her for a few awkward moments. "Would you like to see it?"

The detective nodded, following her out of the gift shop and up the stairs to the third floor.

Bright blue painter's tape still stretched across the opening. Misty's sign stated, "Do not enter—maintenance!" She'd repeated the instructions in Spanish underneath.

Detective Bloyer merely grunted when he saw the door. He stood in the middle of the hallway, staring at it for a few moments while Lydia waited. Then he gestured for her to come forward and unlock the room, though he didn't remove the tape.

The room looked normal to Lydia. It was in the front corner of the building, with drawn shades over the windows that faced east. The bed was just to the right of the door and dominated the space in the room.

The room was still obviously occupied by a guest, as a suitcase lay open on the desk, the TV wasn't flat against the wall but pulled out and turned so that someone on the bed could more easily watch it, and towels (that were probably still wet, dang it!) were resting on the floor just inside the door.

The only odd thing that Lydia noticed was that a candleholder had been placed very carefully on the desk. It was painted with what looked like a Virgin Mary. She sniffed the air, but couldn't smell if the candle had been lit or not.

That was strictly against the rules of the B&B. She might have kicked Ricky out if she'd known about the candle before.

"Where's the spare key?" Detective Bloyer asked after a few moments.

"In a locked box, in the laundry room, which is also generally locked," Lydia said. She did try to keep the laundry room locked.

"And the master?" he said, still looking around the room but not venturing past Misty's sign, which still hung across the doorway.

"There's one in the lockbox," Lydia said, listing them off. "I have one, Misty has one, and Alice has one."

The detective turned to look at her, one eyebrow raised, but he didn't say anything.

Lydia didn't bother replying. Sure, Alice had some developmental issues. She also understood that the master key wasn't something she should give to other people, or even show to them. She only got to use it when she was working.

Admittedly, Alice had lost her keys a few weeks before, at the start of August. Poor girl had been devastated. She'd come to Lydia in tears, not sure where her keys were.

According to Alice's mom, Jen McGowen, it was the first time that Alice had lost her keys in years, possibly even a decade. Lydia wasn't about to try to explain that to the detective though. Alice had been accused of the last murder that had happened in Lake Hope, namely of Schooner Thomas, the former high school principal. Lydia didn't want Alice to be involved in this murder in the slightest.

She really did need to get all the locks in all the rooms changed. Maybe next week she could find some time to schedule an appointment with a locksmith...

Finally, the detective nodded and turned to go back down the stairs.

"What happens next?" Lydia asked as she hurriedly locked the door and started down the stairs after him.

"I need to write up my report," Detective Bloyer said. "Then I can release the room to the next of kin."

"When will you do that?" Lydia said, her gut suddenly hollowing out.

The detective didn't answer until after he'd reached the bottom of the stairs. "I'll be sure to release it as quickly as humanly possible," he assured her.

"Fine," Lydia said, trying to hide her resentment. She could tell that the detective planned on being an asshole just because she hadn't been able to see to him right away when he'd first arrived.

He probably wasn't going to release the room for a week. Maybe more. She was going to be one room short during in the middle of the busy season. Were there any other rooms she could rent for the guests who were coming that week? As well as the week following? Or was all of Lake Hope booked, as usually happened during the busy season?

"Here's my card," the detective said. "I'll be in touch," he added as he walked out the door.

Lydia resisted the urge to crumple the card into a hard ball and throw it at the back of the slowly retreating detective.

He was going to get back at her for making him wait earlier. Lydia couldn't have helped it, though. He'd come in during the middle of lunch rush! On a Saturday, when they were usually busy!

And what was up with Patrice? Why had she had a restraining order out on Ricky? Why hadn't she said something? Lydia would have turned down Ricky's reservation if she'd known.

With a sigh, Lydia went back into the restaurant and started cleaning, carrying empty dishes to the kitchen.

She now understood why Ellis had referred to the officer as "Detective Blowhard." He was really obnoxious.

How long would he keep that room off the market? Lydia remembered fearing that it would be weeks or months—possibly until the end of the year.

No, she wasn't about to allow him to do that to her!

She was just going to have to solve this murder mystery. In three days. Or else.

At least she wasn't going to have to do it completely on her own.

Lydia had a lot of friends.

As did Misty.

5

*L*ydia tried not to use Misty's network unless she was in a real bind.

Like now.

Lydia walked into the kitchen as Misty was rinsing off the cutting boards and knives, putting them into the rack for the sanitizer. She wore a pretty pink blouse that brightened Lydia's spirits just seeing it. She also wore shorts and sandals—it was August and far too hot to wear long pants.

Maybe that had been part of why the detective had been in such a bad mood. He was wearing a suit in all this heat.

Or maybe he was just an asshole.

Lydia put down the plates in the sink, then leaned against the counter. The kitchen was one of her favorite rooms in the B&B. When she'd renovated the building, she'd put in a three-foot-square grill that was perfect for breakfasts, along with an industrial oven for those times she actually baked. The counter that Lydia leaned against had a built-in cutting board that took up much of the surface. Past the stove was a huge walk-in refrigerator. She had only a small freezer, as she was determined to serve fresh food.

One of the tenets that Lydia ran her B&B by was that she never served anything that she wouldn't enjoy herself. It was why she paid more for her coffee beans. Sure, there was cheaper stuff she could get, but if she wouldn't drink it, why should she serve it to her guests?

Finally, Misty looked up from her dishes. "Yes?" she inquired.

"What can you tell me about Detective Joseph Bloyer?" Lydia asked. "And I'd also like to hear everything you know about our former guest, Ricky Hollingsworth."

The grin Misty gave Lydia lit up the entire kitchen. "Well, since you asked…" Misty teased. She pushed a tray of dishes into the sanitizer, pulled the hood down, and set the cycle running.

Lydia stepped up to the sink and started filling the next tray with lunch dishes.

"Detective Bloyer is a transfer from another precinct, out in Walla Walla," Misty said. "He has a good record closing cases. However, he isn't well liked. The impression I got was that his old CO put him up for the transfer to get him out of the department, rather than having to deal with the issue."

Lydia sighed. Of course. It was so much easier to ignore the problem rather than fix it.

"All right, what else can you tell me about him?" Lydia said as she rinsed plates. "Married? Divorced?"

"Divorced, no kids. No problems with excessive

violence," Misty ticked off. "He isn't a bad detective. But I'm not sure that he's a good one, either."

Lydia nodded. "He isn't going to release Ricky's room until after he writes up his report. And who knows how long that will be?"

"Really?" Misty said. She sounded angry.

"Really," Lydia said. "We're going to have to move guests around. Put them up in other places. If there's anywhere in town to put them."

"No, you just wait," Misty said. She already had her phone out.

Lydia kept her smile to herself and just continued rinsing dishes and putting them into the tray while Misty chatted happily in Spanish to someone. Misty had cousins or other relatives pretty much everywhere, including the Yakima police department.

"As the murder didn't occur in the room, it should be released to the next of kin sometime on Monday," Misty said, sounding satisfied.

"Thank you," Lydia said earnestly. "That helps a lot." Even if it took all day, she'd still have the room back before Tuesday, when she needed to turn it over for the next guests.

She would also make a backup plan, though, and see if there was someplace else in town where she could stash someone for a couple of nights.

"What about Ricky?" Lydia prompted as Misty pulled open the hood on the sanitizer and dragged out the tray she'd put in.

"Ricky has two ex-wives, along with a soon-to-be ex,"

Misty said. She blew on the dishes, as they were currently too hot to pick up.

Lydia couldn't help but smile. Misty always blew on the dishes when she was in a hurry. It didn't help cool them at all, but it made her feel better.

"Any chance the current wife did it?" Lydia asked.

"Nope," Misty announced. "She's a wedding photographer and was at a shoot all day."

Lydia nodded. Though it was slightly unusual for a wedding to occur on a Friday, it did happen. "I know that Mr. Hollingsworth wasn't the happiest individual," she said, using the phrase that Misty had used the day before. "Who else might have been unhappy with him?"

"Besides everyone?" Misty said with a grin. "I'm not sure. His ex's aren't garnishing his wages, so I figure he's making child support and alimony. To them, he's worth more alive than dead."

Lydia hesitated, then finally asked, "What about Patrice?"

"She isn't the only woman with a restraining order against Ricky," Misty said. She held up her hand before Lydia could say anything. "I know, I know. I would have said something if I'd known earlier."

That made Lydia feel better, that Misty's broad network hadn't warned her before Ricky showed up. They really hadn't had any idea of the sort of person they were dealing with.

"Who else should we be talking with?" Lydia said, curious what else Misty had found out.

Misty shrugged. "There's a whole lot of people who were angry with Mr. Hollingsworth, even though he only came through town once a year or so," she said. "I would start with Patrice, though. Find out why she had a restraining order out on him."

Lydia nodded grimly. This wasn't a conversation that she wanted to have with her best friend. However, it was necessary, if she was going to solve this case before Detective Blowhard.

6

*L*ydia walked up Main Street to *The Palace*, Patrice's bakery. Like Lydia, Patrice had been shown a lot of local support, helping her stay afloat. Her husband Dan worked as a long-distance trucker, driving a huge semi up and down the west coast for a national shipping company, and he hadn't seen a slowdown at all. So though money had gotten tight for the pair of them, they hadn't been desperate.

Patrice had had to cut back Gracie's hours, which had gotten her to finally move forward with her own pot pie business.

Though it was a lousy time to start a new venture, Gracie had done very well for herself. She made pot pies that were mostly baked, then froze them, for people to reheat at home. They'd become very popular, particularly after she was featured in one of the big tourist magazines.

So in addition to the amazing pastries and cakes that Patrice made, they now had an additional display section with fresh versions of the pot pies. Lydia had to admit that every now and again, having a warm, fresh, chicken pot pie had made her evening.

The Palace smelled like nutmeg and cardamom when Lydia walked in, the bell hanging from the lintel ringing merrily. The display case at the front of the store was mostly empty, as it was close to three o'clock, when Patrice now closed the bakery. She used to keep longer hours, but that was when she'd had a full-time worker to help.

Patrice stood behind the case and nodded to Lydia as she finished explaining with exaggerated patience the ingredients in the apple crumble.

"So it's gluten free?" the woman asked. She sounded frustrated. She looked like a tourist, tall and lanky, with a blue striped short sleeved shirt, white shorts, and flipflops. She had long dirty-blond hair that had been wrapped up into a bun, then artfully held in place by two black and red chopsticks. A large professional-looking camera hung around her neck, and she had a camera bag slung over one shoulder.

Lydia had met her type more than once. The person who considered themselves an *artiste* before all else, and therefore couldn't be held responsible for anything as inconsequential as paying their guest bills.

"Yes, it is," Patrice said. "But I can't guarantee that there is no cross contamination. This isn't a gluten-free bakery. I just try to have at least one gluten- and grain-free selection for people."

Since Patrice had started catering more to the locals than to tourists, she'd expanded her offerings, as it turned out that there were more than one person in town who would buy gluten-free goodies.

And the way that Patrice baked, no one could tell that they weren't full of wheat flour, dairy, or eggs.

Lydia had actually become very fond of one of the gluten- and grain-free cookies that Patrice did. They were more like a shortbread, made from almond flour, hazelnuts, and rosemary.

"I'll take a chance," the woman said, paying for her treat then leaving.

"Want to flip the sign?" Patrice asked Lydia as soon as the woman left.

Lydia walked to the door and flipped over the sign, showing that the bakery was now closed. She also turned off the neon "Open" sign that lighted the window next to the door, then helped Patrice bus and clear the two tables that were in the bakery.

Like Lydia, Patrice had removed some of the seating from her establishment, then decided that she actually preferred having fewer customers in the shop at once.

"The outdoor seating's already been cleared," Patrice told Lydia as she handed her a spray bottle of disinfectant.

Lydia grimaced but dutifully sprayed the tabletops, wiping them clean, along with the seats and backs of the chairs. The smell of bleach and alcohol was something she'd just had to get used to.

As Lydia finished her section, Patrice cleaned off the door, the display cases, and anything else that her customers might have touched.

Finally, the pair of friends finished and walked back behind the counter, into the kitchen, Patrice's domain.

"Can I get you anything?" Patrice asked as she stowed away the cleaning supplies.

"I wouldn't say no to a ginger molasses cookie," Lydia admitted.

"And a cup of coffee?" Patrice said as she poured herself some.

"Decaf, please," Lydia said. Though Patrice liked her coffee a bit darker than Lydia, it was still awfully good.

But the main reason she liked it darker was so that way she could sweeten it up some, and still have it taste like coffee. Lydia had teased her friend more than once about how she just liked coffee-flavored milk and honey, while Lydia tended to take hers black.

Patrice still kept a couple of folding chairs in the kitchen so friends could visit and they could chat. However, she now wore a mask whenever she baked, and insisted that anyone who visited do the same when she was cooking.

Lydia pulled out a folding chair and sat near the door. Patrice leaned against one of the stainless steel counters that ran along the edges of the room. She looked tired, Lydia realized.

Patrice always looked stunning, her golden frizzy hair threatening to escape the careful bun at the back of her head. As usual, her makeup was flawless, with just a touch of eyeliner to highlight her large blue eyes, her lips painted a soft shade of red.

But there were dark circles under her eyes. Her white skin looked paler than usual. And Lydia recognized the worry lines around her friend's mouth, as she'd developed some of her own that past year.

"I suppose you want to know about Ricky," Patrice said.

"Yes," Lydia said immediately. "I'm sorry—"

"You didn't know," Patrice said. "I hadn't told you about it. I had just thought that Ricky was being weird. It wasn't until the last month or so that it got icky. Which was after you'd already accepted the reservation."

"I still would have canceled if you'd said something," Lydia said hotly. She wouldn't have liked doing it. She really didn't like disappointing people. However, she would have been able to fill the spot, as it was August and the height of tourist season.

"I know," Patrice said, nodding. "It just felt like an imposition."

Lydia stood right up and walked over to Patrice, reaching out for her friend's hands. "It would have been fine," she insisted, squeezing Patrice's hands tightly. "You're not weak for wanting some sort of protection."

That at least got Lydia a fragile smile. "I know." She squeezed Lydia's hands back. "I do know that." She sighed. "It was Dan who insisted on the restraining order. Particularly since he had to be traveling this week."

"So what happened?" Lydia asked, going back to her seat. She took a nibble on her amazing cookie, followed by a sip of coffee. Such a comfort, which she knew she'd need, given the look on her friend's face.

"It started out innocently enough," Patrice said. "He started following the bakery on social media, liking and loving everything I posted. There were some weird comments, like how 'the sweet' was providing sweets. I just figured it was awkward socialization. You know?"

Lydia nodded. She'd seen more than one tourist who was just awkward, not creepy. "But they struck you as off, didn't they?"

Patrice nodded grimly. She took a gulp of her own coffee, as if clearing away a bad taste in her mouth. "When the comments got too personal—and too weird—I finally blocked him. Fake accounts started following me, and the comments were too similar for me not to think it was the same guy."

"For how long?" Lydia asked.

"It started last year, after his tour through here," Patrice said. "He gave an outdoor concert, remember?"

Lydia shook her head. She did remember *The Cove* had expanded their "beer garden" the previous summer and had held some concerts there.

"Around March, everything calmed down. I was only having a crazy comment once a week, instead of three or four a day," Patrice said. "It was a quiet period. I'd just hoped he'd go away."

"But he didn't," Lydia prompted.

Patrice sighed. "But he didn't. Instead of following me online, he started showing up at the bakery once or twice a month, starting in June. He must have followed me home at some point, because I found him sitting across the street in his car, with binoculars, watching the house."

Lydia shivered. That sounded just awful.

"He was one of those men who wouldn't take 'no' as an answer. That was just a challenge to him. I don't know why he thought I'd be interested in him. I never gave him any indication that I was," Patrice said.

"You know that his obsession wasn't necessarily about you, right?" Lydia said.

"I know," Patrice said, nodding. "Then he started coming in here every day. Or he'd be sitting across the street, watching me through the window. His comments were getting threatening, too. He'd accuse me of 'cheating' on him when I was nice to a male customer."

Patrice shivered, her arms wrapped around her torso.

"I'm so sorry," Lydia said. "That must have been awful for you." She wanted to give her friend a hug, but knew that it wouldn't be welcome. Not at this point.

"So I had to take out the restraining order, so he would stop coming into the bakery. That was only a few weeks ago. I wasn't looking forward to him being here. But I figured I was safe enough. Gracie or Dan were always here to walk me to my car." Patrice paused. "I'm not glad that Ricky died. But I am glad that he isn't bothering me anymore."

"I really wish you would have told me," Lydia said.

"I do too," Patrice told her. "I just...I didn't want to be a bother."

"It wouldn't have been a bother," Lydia said. "This man was threatening you. You deserve to be protected."

"I know," Patrice said. "I'm...I'm talking with someone about the whole incident."

"Good," Lydia said firmly. "And you can call me if you need to talk, or need a shoulder to cry on, or someone to vent to, or even to just come over and drink some wine."

"I'd like that," Patrice said with a soft smile. "This whole thing—it was one more stress on top of everything else that I just didn't need, you know?"

"I hear you," Lydia said. "So what now?"

Patrice shook her head. "I've already had to talk with the detective, once." She grimaced. "He didn't believe me when I told him I had nothing to do with it. He thinks that you arranged the wine tour so that I could be there to stab Ricky."

Lydia snorted. "That's ridiculous."

"Well, I know that's ridiculous, and you know that's ridiculous. But that detective? Not so much," Patrice said. She took another sip of her coffee. "However, I didn't do it. You believe me, right?"

"Of course," Lydia said. "You wouldn't have stabbed a man with a thermometer. You might have missed his heart. You would have taken him out using one of your knives."

Patrice gave Lydia a big grin. "Exactly. Why use an instrument that may only injure your intended victim?" Then she sobered. "However, that sort of blood-thirsty attitude won't go very far with the detective."

"I know," Lydia said. "And you know that if I could give you an alibi I would, right?"

"I do know," Patrice said. "And thank you. The same goes for you, if you should need help."

"Friends help friends move. Real friends help move bodies," Lydia joked.

"Exactly!" Patrice said.

"You know this means we're going to have to solve the case ourselves, right?" Lydia inquired after taking another nibble of her absolutely delicious cookie.

"I might have an idea already," Patrice said. She paused, then added, "You're probably not going to like it."

Lydia grimaced. "Would it be better than my best friend going to jail?"

"Probably," Patrice said.

Lydia had to giggle. Through all the stress and strain of the past year, it was nice to just have girl time again. Even if it involved catching a murderer.

7

*A*fter her long chat with Patrice, Lydia hurried back to the B&B. As she entered her domain, she saw Misty in the gift shop, talking with some guests.

Good. Lydia had purposefully let the inventory run low on some of the items in her gift shop. Hopefully, she'd have to stock up again soon.

However, before Lydia could escape back into the kitchen, or her apartment, she saw that someone was sitting in the dining area.

"I'm sorry," Lydia said stepping forward. "This area—why, hi, Mom. What are you doing here?"

Helen Marsh stood up, turned, and smiled at her daughter. "Hello, dear," she said. "I was stealing your space to stuff some envelopes with political fliers."

Lydia had been proud of her mom while she'd been growing up (teenage years of hating everything and everyone not withstanding). Helen was tall like her husband Emerson, but not as lean as Lydia. She had dark hair that had gone gray gradually, and she wore it in a cute pixie cut.

That afternoon, she was in what Ed and Alan would call "office worker chic" with an off-white blouse that had gold trim, plain black pants, and gray Chuck Taylor sneakers that really pulled the look together. She had on more makeup than usual, smoothing out her wrinkles and accentuating her large hazel eyes.

"All right," Lydia said, noticing that indeed, her mother had pushed together two tables in the center of the restaurant, filling each with pamphlets. The procedure was obvious: someone would walk around the table, picking up one of each pamphlet and stuffing them into an envelope, before sealing it and applying an address sticker.

"I was just taking a break before starting the next batch," Mom continued. "You weren't here, but Misty said that you weren't using the space for anything."

Lydia nodded. "It's fine," she said. "But you know that I can't put up any of those pamphlets, right?"

"I know. You've explained before how you can't support your own dear mother," Helen said with exaggerated angst.

Lydia couldn't help but roll her eyes. Her mom had been pretty conservative while she'd been working. Since she'd retired, she'd definitely loosened up.

Which made her a much more interesting candidate than her opponent.

"So tell me the latest gossip," Mom said as she started walking around the table again, picking up pamphlets.

Lydia waited a couple of beats before she followed

along. She wouldn't be able to do too much—she had to start getting tomorrow's breakfast prepped. But she could help her mom for a while. Plus, it gave them an excuse to chat.

So Lydia told her mom about Ricky, how he'd been killed, how she needed to solve the case so she could get the room back. She mentioned that Ricky wasn't the best person, as there had been several women who'd had restraining orders out on him.

Mom sighed at that. "On the one hand, we need our laws. We need to maintain ourselves as a lawful society. On the other hand, that sort of pattern should have raised a *lot* of red flags. I wish he'd been able to get help before it came to this."

Lydia nodded. As her mom had worked in one of the more honest law firms in town, they'd done a lot of pro-bono work for women who'd needed help with divorces and such. So she was familiar with some of the problems women ran into.

"How's Theo doing?" Lydia asked after a few moments of comfortable silence. While Lydia and her brother had gotten closer since he'd come out as bisexual, they still weren't close. She rarely talked with him on the phone. She did try to remember, at least once a month, to text him and see how he was doing.

His new lifestyle, as well as his new boyfriend Steve, seemed to make everything better.

Mom's grin at the question lit up the whole area. "Theo's doing so much better now. Steve is such a dear. And so good with Theo's boy!"

Lydia was looking forward to Christmas that year, and spending time with her entire family. "I'm happy for them," she said. The statement came out a little more wistful than she'd planned.

"Trouble in paradise?" Mom asked quietly.

Lydia shrugged. "It's a long-distance relationship," she said. "We're both trying to make it work."

"Is it working, though?" Mom questioned.

"I don't know," Lydia said, being honest. "There are times when we get along great. But other times when we don't."

"I see," Mom said. "Are the good times good enough to tide you over the bad times?"

"I'm not sure," Lydia said. And that was really the sticking point. She really liked Ellis. Possibly even loved him.

But how in love was she with him? She couldn't say.

"It will all work out in the end," Mom assured her daughter. "And you know we're here to support you, no matter what, right?"

"I know," Lydia said. "And I'm still so grateful to the pair of you."

Mom smiled and nodded. "You'll be fine. Although, you might feel better if you had at least a few pamphlets around. Just to show your support of your family…"

Lydia snorted. "No, I wouldn't. But that was a good try. Sneaky, like."

The mischievous grin Mom gave made Lydia take a step back. "Oh, I have much more sneaky plans being developed, even as we speak. I intend to win this election."

"Then what?" Lydia asked, unsurprised that her mom was pursuing politics. She'd been the power behind the throne for most of her career. It was about time she got into the limelight.

"There might be a seat on the Water Board that I have my eye on," Mom admitted. "There aren't many positions out here that I could run for, though. So we might just have to move. Or establish a second residence."

Lydia nodded slowly. She didn't want her parents to leave Lake Hope. She drew a lot of comfort with them out there. However, she did understand that they might not always want to live out on a hobby farm with all the upkeep it required.

"I'd miss you," Lydia admitted.

"It's a long way off," Mom admitted. "But before I apply for a larger, more prestigious position, I'm going to need to prove myself on the smaller stage."

"All right," Lydia said, though she had a feeling that her mother was leading up to something.

"One of the skills that a good candidate should have is the ability to debate their opponent," Mom said, still sounding overtly casual.

"Okay…" Lydia said, waiting for the other shoe to drop.

"Now, I know that you can't overtly support one candidate over another. But you would help your mom if you could, right?"

"Of course," Lydia said.

"Good!" Mom said. "Then you wouldn't mind if I debated my opponent here, right?"

She handed Lydia one of the pamphlets. It already announced the debate on Sunday evening, though the location was yet to be determined.

Lydia thought for a moment. Sunday nights tended to be pretty dead around here. She'd have some prep to do for Monday morning, but Misty could help with that.

"You can have your debate here," Lydia said. "Where would you have gone if I'd said no?" she asked as she handed the pamphlet back.

Mom walked back around the table and picked up two pages, then handed them to Lydia.

One announced the location of the debate as the *Nip and Bud*. The other announced that it would take place at *The Cove*.

"Have you talked with Toby?" Lydia said. She'd gotten to know the owner of *The Cove* better since the year before, when she'd gotten the person who'd murdered Schooner Thomas to confess while drinking in the bar.

"No," Mom said. "He was my next stop. I figured they might want an audience or something, since they've had to cancel Ricky's gig."

That made sense. However, Lydia knew that the usual crowd at *The Cove* were likely to be rowdier. It was more of a drinking bar than a political salon.

"No, I want you to be here," Lydia said after a moment. She suspected that her mom would draw a much larger crowd at the *Nip and Bud*. Then Lydia gave her mom a hard stare. "That way, I can keep my eye on you," she teased.

Mom giggled. "Thank you. Have I mentioned tonight that I'm proud of you? Of all that you've accomplished?"

Lydia smiled, then walked into the open arms of her mother.

Sure, things might be a little rough around the edges still. But she still had her family. Her home.

Everything was going to be all right.

8

*L*ater that evening, Lydia sat in her living room, firmly ensconced in her wingback chair, reading a fun, if kind of silly, action adventure thriller that took place in Seattle. She generally only allowed herself a single glass of wine in the evening, so it had better be pretty good wine. Tonight's was from one of her favorite vineyard's, Blue Pond, a nice, light Sangiovese that she served slightly chilled. It was light enough to be refreshing, but hearty enough to be satisfying.

Lydia could never taste all the "berry, citrus, and floral" notes in a wine, no matter how many times she listened to winemakers talk about their product. However, she did know what she liked, and was lucky enough to be able to get a discount on some of her favorites.

Her living room felt very cozy that evening. The lamps in the corner highlighted the golden wood of the ceiling. The smell of the wine warmed everything up. It was a touch cool—the window in the bedroom was already open, letting in the evening breezes. But Lydia preferred it that way.

Lydia was just taking a break from her book, debating maybe having another half glass of wine, when her phone rang. She smiled when she saw that it was Ellis. "Hi there," she said as she stretched out her legs. Oooff. She'd been sitting too long.

"Why, hello," Ellis said in that deep, smooth voice of his. "How are you?"

"Hanging in there," Lydia said as she bent over, stretching out her back and legs. "How are you? What have you been up to?"

Ellis chatted about his morning run, mentioning that he had a new case, but it seemed to be more gathering existing evidence than trying to solve a crime plotted by a mastermind.

He didn't give her any details, of course. He really couldn't talk about his work. She understood, though it bothered her sometimes.

Lydia told him of her mom and hosting the debate. Ellis chuckled. "You should arrange to do a wine tasting that night as well. Could really make some money."

Lydia pressed her lips together instead of correcting him. Sure, she made a little bit of extra cash by holding wine tastings. However, that wasn't why she did it. It was to highlight the local vineyards, to give those who didn't have a popular tasting room the chance to sell more bottles to tourists. She was a part of her community, and the wine tastings were as much about showing off that community as anything else.

"I also talked to Patrice about Ricky," Lydia said.

"Oh?" Ellis said.

"She had a restraining order out against him," Lydia said.

"I know," Ellis said. He sounded curt, as if he didn't want her to say anything more.

"I met Detective Blowhard," Lydia said, trying to lighten the mood.

"Please don't call him that. I shouldn't have used that name," Ellis said.

"It's an accurate description," Lydia said. She started pacing across the floor of her small living room. Normally, it was perfectly sized for her. Right now, though, it felt cramped. The purple micro-suede loveseat stuck out too far. The noise of the refrigerator humming to itself suddenly irritated her.

"It might be," Ellis said. "But I have to work with the man. And I can't use that name regularly, or I might make the mistake and call him that to his face."

"All right," Lydia said, relenting. "Did you know that he was deliberately delaying releasing the room back to me?"

"He wasn't. He wouldn't do such a thing," Ellis said, automatically defending his coworker.

"Yeah, he was," Lydia said. "At least according to Misty."

Ellis sighed. "Let's not talk about this."

"Then what should we talk about?" Lydia snapped. "This is *the* big thing that's going on in my life. And if I don't get that room back, I'm going to have to not only find another place to put those guests, I'm going to end up paying for it."

"I know, this affects your livelihood," Ellis said, trying to be soothing. "But this is my job as well. And I really cannot share the details of anything I may know about the case."

It was Lydia's turn to sigh. "I do know that. It's just frustrating sometimes. Particularly now. Because I can't talk with you about what I'm going to do tomorrow."

"What are you going to do tomorrow?" Ellis asked cautiously.

"I really can't talk to you about it," Lydia said. She was partially teasing, partially still pissed off. But she didn't want some defense attorney getting the case thrown out of court because she'd prejudiced a witness.

Or even the murderer herself.

"As long as you'll be safe," Ellis warned. "Promise me that."

"I'll be as safe as I can be," Lydia said.

After a few moments of awkward silence, Ellis finally said, "I'll, uh, talk with you later. Okay? Sweet dreams."

"Sweet dreams for you too," Lydia replied automatically before she hung up.

She stood there in the middle of her beautiful space, staring at her phone, before tossing it to the side and walking over to her fridge.

Though she hadn't planned on having a second glass of wine that night, it sure sounded good right now.

She thought again about the question her mom had asked her earlier that evening. Did the good times that she and Ellis had together outweigh the bad?

More and more, that answer was looking like *no*.

9

After Lydia and Misty had finished serving both breakfast and lunch Sunday morning, Lydia went back into her rooms to change clothes before her appointment.

She'd arranged to meet Jennifer Lee, the widow of Ricky Hollingsworth, later that afternoon. Lydia was pretending to be newly engaged and interviewing different wedding photographers.

It had surprised her to find out that Ricky and his wife only lived about thirty minutes away, north of Lake Hope, in a small town called Benson. She'd figured they'd live in a larger city.

However, according to Jennifer's website—Ring of Fire Photography—she'd drive anywhere in the state of Washington to get the perfect photograph for you.

The day was clear and hot. Lydia finally settled on a nice sleeveless blouse made out of a soft, light-blue material that made her gray eyes look much bluer. She didn't bother with makeup—that really wasn't who she was. She added a pair of dark blue stretchy shorts, with gladiator style sandals that had crossing straps halfway up her calves.

She didn't want to leave her hair down—it was far too hot for that. She did add bobby pins that had little hearts on the ends to her hair. That was as about as romantic as she normally got. Besides, they were cute. And Ed and Alan approved of them.

She didn't have an engagement ring, but she figured that was all right. Her cover story was that she and her fiancé were having custom rings made, so it would be another couple of weeks before she had her ring.

It had been Patrice's idea that Lydia should go and talk to Ricky's widow, to see if she had any idea about who'd killed her husband.

According to Misty, Ricky and Jennifer had been fighting a lot. They had been living closer to Spokane, but had moved earlier that year to Benson.

The timing coincided with Patrice's story: the couple had been selling their house and buying a new one during the time Ricky had stopped bothering Patrice as much.

Once they'd moved, Ricky had started showing up on Patrice's doorstep. Lydia would bet that the days when he'd come down to Lake Hope were the days that his wife was out on photoshoots and had no idea where he was.

Lydia took the scenic drive up to Benson, leaving with plenty of time as there were sure to be tourists (and possibly tour buses) on the two-lane highway. Fortunately, the buses trundled off the road going to various vineyards whenever she felt a bit too slowed down.

Jennifer and Ricky lived on the edge of town, that

outer ring that divided the farmland from the houses crowded together. They had a corner lot. Their property backed up onto a field with cows lazing, and across the street was another farm. However, following the street going into town were more houses.

The Ring of Fire Photography studio was located in a small shed that had been built at the front of the property. While an asphalt driveway led to the house itself, a smaller, gravel driveway led to the shed. The studio building was painted a lovely bright green that stood out against the brown, dried grass of the yard. The shed was probably twelve feet by sixteen feet, a single story high, with a rounded roof, like a tiny barn.

Lydia pulled up the gravel driveway and parked her car right in front of the shed. A woman came out just a few moments later.

She was tall, like Lydia. She had bangs, but also longish sandy-blonde hair that she wore up in a bun, held in place by a single green and gold chopstick. She was skinny, dressed in a sleeveless red cotton camisole that had a second black camisole underneath it. The shorts she wore were a khaki green color and she was barefoot. A large golden cross hung from a chain around her neck.

For a moment, she looked familiar. Had Lydia seen Jennifer in town at some point?

"Thanks for coming out to see me!" Jennifer said as she walked over. She winced a bit, but kept walking.

Gravel covered all the ground in front of the studio. Why hadn't the woman put on shoes?

"Thank you for seeing me on such short notice," Lydia said. She'd honestly been surprised, when she'd called

Jennifer, that the photographer had suggested that they meet the next day.

Shouldn't she be in mourning for her husband? Or did she need the work to keep her going?

"Sure," Jennifer said with a grin.

Lydia looked at Jennifer, then shook her head. "You look so familiar," she said. "I live in Lake Hope, just south of here. I run a B&B there, and the *Nip and Bud* tea shop. Have you ever been there?"

"No, ma'am," Jennifer said. "We just moved to the area a few months ago. Still trying to find all the great places!"

Lydia nodded. She could tell that the other woman's cheer was pasted on. Her smile never actually reached her eyes.

"I won't take up too much of your time, I promise," Lydia said, hoping that would soothe the person in front of her.

"It's all right," Jennifer said, determinedly. "I've recently lost my husband," she confided. "I need to work. I need to stay busy."

"Oh, how tragic!" Lydia said. "You poor dear!" She didn't mind laying it on a bit thick. She needed to get Jennifer to trust her.

Jennifer just shrugged. "It was so sudden, you know?" she said. "But when the Lord calls us back, you have to answer."

"I'm surprised you're seeing me on a Sunday," Lydia said, hesitatingly.

Jennifer looked at Lydia with big eyes. "I know. But the Lord told me I should see you right away."

"Okay," Lydia said, not sure how to respond.

"Come into my office," Jennifer said, turning away. "I have AC."

"That would be lovely," Lydia said, following her into the small shed, wincing every time Jennifer stepped wrong on the hard rocks and winced herself.

The inside of the photography studio was delightfully cool, but the air reeked of patchouli and candle wax. Just inside the door, on the right, was a small desk with two plain folding chairs in front of it and an ergonomically designed office chair behind it. An ancient computer monitor took up the far corner of the desk, and papers were strewn across the surface of it.

Windows took up most of the walls. Every single window ledge held at least half a dozen (or more) glass candle holders. Lydia couldn't see the figures painted on all of them, but the candles closest to her were covered in painted pictures of the Virgin Mary.

They reminded her of the one she'd seen in Ricky's room.

"Please, sit," Jennifer said, indicating one of the folding chairs. "Can I get you anything? Water? Tea? Coffee?"

Lydia cautiously sat after checking to make sure there wasn't candle wax on the seat. "No, I'm fine, thank you," she said.

While Jennifer shuffled through some of the papers on her desk, obviously looking for something, Lydia continued looking around.

Behind the desk, in the opposite corner, was a four-foot-wide screen that had a screen saver showing pictures of different weddings. The "ring of fire" technique was obvious in most of them. It showed a bride and a groom leaning toward each other, and a light flare where their lips were about to meet. The same technique had been used with couples showing off their rings, a bright circle of light connecting the two.

Lydia suddenly knew that if she ever decided to get married again, she was never having someone like Jennifer take the pictures. They were too artful, too staged. The ring of fire technique was being used to fake the emotion that the couples should exude.

The pictures were absolutely beautiful. But where was the heart?

"Here it is!" Jennifer said, finally dislodging a brochure from under yet another stack of disorganized papers. "This details all the packages that I offer couples."

"Thank you," Lydia said, taking it. She resisted the temptation to wipe her fingers against her bare thighs after touching the slightly greasy paper.

Had Jennifer used it for a napkin with a fatty burger?

The prices made Lydia gulp. They seemed way high to her. Then again, she'd never used a photographer. All the pictures of the B&B were professionally done by Freddie, who updated them every year for Lydia. However, Freddie worked in exchange for free use of one of the rooms for her parents when they came to town. It was a great bargain as far as Lydia was concerned, not having to put the money up front. And Freddie's parents loved the B&B— they probably would have stayed there even if it weren't free for them.

Comparatively, Jennifer's prices were at least a third higher than the cost of a room.

Was Freddie giving Lydia that much of a discount? She was afraid to ask, afraid that Freddie might raise her prices...

Instead of focusing on the cost, Lydia looked at the pictures. At least in the brochure, there appeared to be some actual emotion captured: a bride and her bridesmaids all laughing together; a couple holding hands, facing each other, their foreheads touching; and the grand event, with a tiny little ring bearer walking toward the happy couple in the distance, rose petals scattered across the aisle.

"These are beautiful," Lydia said honestly.

"Thank you," Jennifer said. "It's my job to capture the perfect moments of your most important day."

Lydia worked hard not to roll her eyes at the obvious marketing speak. "We're thinking of something a bit smaller, more intimate," she said as she put the brochure to the side. "This isn't the first marriage for either of us."

"Didn't learn the first time, eh?" Jennifer joked. "How many would be in your wedding party?"

"Probably just me and a single maid of honor," Lydia said. Of course, she'd have Patrice in her wedding.

"Are you sure? Don't you want more people there to celebrate with you? To witness your sacred vows?" Jennifer said.

"Well, maybe," Lydia said. She knew that Alice would love being part of a wedding party. As would Misty.

"Good, good," Jennifer said. "It's really important to have many people with you on such an important occasion. To remind you why you're so happy together with your husband, at least at that moment."

"Is that why you take pictures of weddings? To remind you of your happiness?" Lydia asked, ignoring the implication that Jennifer was making, that Lydia wouldn't always be happy with her husband.

"Exactly," Jennifer said. Her eyes grew wide as she started to preach. "Marriage is the most sacred of any union. It is a blessing from the Lord to find your mate. And anyone who breaks those vows shouldn't make them in the first place," she added darkly.

"I know, right?" Lydia said, going with the flow. "My first husband, well, let's just say I was naïve to think that his behavior would change after that first time I caught him cheating," she lied.

Neil had been faithful the entire time they'd been together, she was certain. Being unfaithful would have meant that he'd actually gotten up off his ass and gone and done something, rather than just complaining about it.

"I feel your pain," Jennifer said. She reached across the desk, scattering some of the top papers on the floor. She ignored them and squeezed Lydia's hand uncomfortably tightly.

Jennifer's hands were hot and sweaty, as if she were running a fever.

She held on though. "My husband—my most recent husband—chased after a number of women. Mind you, I don't think it started off as his fault. I think they enticed him. But he was a weak man, and was easily ensnared."

"I see," Lydia said. She sat back in her chair, sliding her

hand away from Jennifer's hot grabby one. "Was he your first husband?"

"No, my third. All of them cheated on me," Jennifer said darkly. She sat back. "I should have listened to the Virgin Mary when she appeared to me in a vision. I knew better than to marry Ricky. But I did anyway, wanting to create that perfect moment."

"I'm so sorry," Lydia said. "That's so awful to have your trust broken like that. More than once!"

"It's all right," Jennifer said, pasting her smile back on. She really could be a pretty woman when she smiled that way. If you could get past the fact that her eyes retained that fervent, crazed look. "Your new man won't treat you badly as mine did," she assured Lydia.

"You're right," Lydia said, nodding. "He's a winemaker. Too busy with his crops to find time to cheat on me!"

"He might be having dalliances with other women in the fields, you know," Jennifer warned. She probably had meant it as teasing, or at least hoped it would come out that way.

"Right," Lydia said, laying on the sarcasm. "In between the sprinklers and the pickers!"

"Exactly," Jennifer said. She gave a deep sigh. "But let's talk more about your perfect day. I suppose you'll get married out at his vineyard?"

"Yes," Lydia said, nodding. "And it's perfectly appropriate! The Heart Vineyards. Have you heard of that?"

Jennifer gave her a strange look. For the first time, a true smile appeared on her face. "Yes. Yes I have," she purred. "It sounds perfect."

Then, like a switch being flipped, Jennifer turned into the consummate professional. She discussed different lighting techniques, noon shots versus late afternoon shots, individual as well as group shots.

Lydia was impressed with the woman's knowledge and felt herself growing more at ease. Jennifer really was a good photographer, even if she was as crazy as a June bug.

By the time she left, Lydia had a much better understanding of what sorts of pictures were possible for a wedding. It was a shame she couldn't put that knowledge to use, as she certainly wasn't about to marry Ellis anytime soon.

She was also certain that Jennifer was hiding something. Possibly several somethings.

And they all revolved around the murder of her husband.

10

*L*ydia didn't have a lot of time when she returned to the B&B to get things ready for the evening's debate.

Though Alice didn't generally work on Sundays, both she and her mom had volunteered to come in and help Lydia prepare. The pair of them walked in the front door as Lydia came walking up from the back.

"Hi there!" Lydia said, glad to see both of them.

Alice was shorter than her mom. Her round face and constantly surprised expression were clear indicators of her developmental condition. Though Alice was in her late twenties, according to her parents, she was mentally between eight and twelve years old. She wore her brightly colored tie-dye T-shirt and jeans, along with her usual big grin.

It was easy to see the familial relationship between mother and daughter, particularly when they were standing side by side. Jen's face was also a bit round, and they shared the same bright blue eyes. Jen's hair had gone prematurely gray, something she teasingly blamed on Alice occasionally. She wore comfortable farm clothing, thick sturdy jeans even in the heat of summer and dark, men's style T-shirts that hid her muscles.

"So, you ready to help your mom win this debate?" Jen asked.

"Oh, no," Lydia said. "I cannot appear to be biased, or I'll lose support from half the town," she warned.

Jen just shrugged. "Then you should lose it," she said. "Alan Turflow is a tool."

Lydia nodded, agreeing. She'd heard a lot about the other lawyers in town while she'd been growing up. Alan had never once impressed her mother with his ethics. He'd never stepped over the line far enough that she could report him to the state bar, but she'd considered it, more than once.

"I'm going to start the coffee," Lydia said. "Could you two move the tables out into the laundry room? Except the long one, which goes next to the tea set wall. Then put out the chairs? Mom rented a bunch. They're over there," Lydia said, pointing to where Misty had stacked them.

"Sure!" Alice said happily. She lifted one of the tables by herself and started walking back toward the laundry room.

Lydia exchanged a smile with Jen. "Thank you again for coming to help," she said.

Jen snorted at her. "I'm not here to help you," she said. "I'm here to make sure that your mom wins the debate."

Then, not to be outdone by her daughter, Jen picked up one of the larger tables by herself and started down the hallway next to the staircase, going to the laundry room.

Lydia shook her head. While she could lift the tables on her own, both of the McGowen women were much stronger than she was.

Instead, she headed back into the kitchen to start preparing coffee. How much should she make? She decided to put decaf in the big urn out front, and have a second one with caffeinated coffee on the side.

What if no one showed up? That would be awful for her mom. Maybe Lydia should have agreed to put a brochure up in the window, so that people walking by would have at least known about the debate. No one could accuse her of playing favorites, not if she had both candidates here at the same time.

Should she charge for the coffee? Maybe she'd just put up a donation basket. No, that wouldn't work. People would just use it for empty napkins and stir sticks.

Then she had an idea. She had a large glass jar that she'd bought pickles in. She cleaned it thoroughly, then, using her sharpest knife, cut a hole in the top of the screw-lid, big enough for folded bills. She taped a sign to the side of it, saying "Coffee donations."

That would have to do. Mom had ordered three dozen cookies from Patrice's bakery to serve. Her opponent hadn't contributed anything, of course.

Lydia put the cookies out on trays, arranging them just so, because that was part of her nature. She wasn't an artist, not really. However, she did like pretty things around her, and so worked to make sure that her everyday life was beautiful.

By the time Lydia had finished setting up the coffee and cookies in the kitchen, Jen and Alice had finished arranging the chairs. It was only then that Lydia remembered that her mom had asked her to also have a table just inside the door, where people could sign their names if they wanted to join a candidate's email list, as well as pick up brochures.

Alice cheerfully went to get the table, which Lydia covered in a cheerful summer-themed tablecloth, with rainbow-colored beach umbrellas and pink and green flipflops decorating the border.

Then she took a step back, trying to look at the place critically. The candidates would be up front, with their backs to the wall with all the tea sets on it. That would at least give people something to look at if they got tired of the debate. The table in front of them needed a plainer tablecloth, and a pitcher of water with glasses for the speakers.

The chairs were all spaced orderly. Possibly precisely. She suspected Alice had a hand in that—she liked things "tidy" as she called them. When she made up the gift baskets that Lydia left in every room—which included soap, chocolate, coffee, and tea—she always insisted on placing the items so that they were symmetrical.

After Lydia finished fixing up the front table, her mom came bustling in. "Oh, my goodness!" she said when she looked around. "You beat me to doing the setup!" she added, glaring at Lydia.

"Blame us," Jen said, stepping forward. Jen and Helen gave each other hugs, and included Alice as well.

While her mom and Jen set up the front table, Alice and Lydia went back into the kitchen. Lydia still had to prep food for Monday's breakfast. She didn't know how long she had before people started arriving, so she worked fast. First she pulled cantaloupe and honeydew from the refrigerator, then she started slicing it up for the fruit salad she'd serve.

"Wow, you're fast," Alice commented after a few moments.

"I've had a lot of practice," Lydia admitted. She'd been cutting up fruit for a salad for breakfast ever since she'd opened the B&B over five years before.

Alice launched into a tale about how she'd learned how to be so careful with a knife, even showing Lydia the scar she had on the knuckle of one hand where she'd sliced herself so badly that she'd had to have stitches.

While Lydia cut fruit and prepared pancake batter for the morning, people started filling into the restaurant. Since her mom and Jen were there, Lydia didn't feel the need to go out front. Everything was set up. People could help themselves.

She'd put a card holder for Patrice's business cards next to the cookies, in case someone hadn't tried them before. Lydia considered it a good practice to advertise the other local businesses. She didn't buy her coffee locally—she honestly didn't care for any of the local roasts—otherwise she would have advertised them as well.

As Lydia was finishing up, Jen stuck her head in the kitchen. "Someone is interested in something in the gift shop," she said.

"Thank you," Lydia said, washing her hands and hurriedly putting away the last of her breakfast prep.

Normally, she would have closed the gift shop. But things had been so tight that she welcomed every chance she got to sell anything, instead of having to carry the stock.

One of the people attending the debate wanted to buy the book about the local ghosts. Another person bought one of the very pretty coaster sets that Lydia had, made out of beautiful local sandstone with trees carved into them.

When Lydia finished with the guests in the gift shop, she finally checked her watch.

The debate was supposed to have started five minutes ago.

However, only her mom was seated at the front of the room. The person moderating the debate was there as well —Connie Spruce, a local radio host, standing to the side and chatting amicably with two other people.

Where was Alan?

Of course, Lydia's mind leaped to the worst possible scenario. Alan had been attacked just before he'd walked into the B&B. When people left, they'd find his body on the street outside.

Lydia shook her head. No, he was probably just being rude.

At ten minutes after the hour, Connie called the room to order. "So it seems that your worthy opponent has decided not to grace us with his presence." Her voice had a soothing quality to it, that made people automatically feel at ease. She wore a bright red blouse that looked fantastic on her. Her makeup was flawless, accenting her high cheekbones and aquiline nose.

Why hadn't she gone into TV broadcasting? She certainly had the looks for it.

"Should I call the debate? Award the win to the only candidate who bothered showing up?" Connie asked.

Before people could respond, Alan came bustling in the door. "I'm sorry I'm so late!" he proclaimed as he hustled toward the table where Lydia's mom and Connie already sat at.

He was a short, round man. He wore cheap suits and even cheaper ties. Even his brown loafers were scuffed. Lydia was surprised they didn't squeak when he walked.

His white face was pasty, and he had a bad comb-over across his bald head. He had a short mustache that looked like a fuzzy worm had just climbed up there and possibly died.

"So gracious of you to join us," Connie said.

The slathering of sarcasm that Connie put over those words was delicious.

"I was still at the office. Working on a case," Alan said as way of his excuse.

Was that supposed to impress people, that he was putting in hours on a Sunday? It just made Lydia more cross. The implication was that his time was so much more important than hers and everyone else's.

Lydia hoped that other people would be just as dead set against him as she was, even before hearing him speak.

But the debate was about letting the candidates talk about their take on the issues of law enforcement and the courts. It was about highlighting their differences, rather than actually convincing anyone.

During the debate, Lydia felt restless, unable to focus. She excused herself and went to the kitchen, taking out her excess energy on thoroughly cleaning the grill and chopping area. She still listened, feeling a warm appreciation for her mother and the way that she approached things, instead of the cold, selfish attitude of Alan's.

Of course, Lydia felt her mom won hands down, particularly after the bad showing Alan had made at the start.

Only time would tell, once the voters went to the polls.

11

Check this out

$\mathcal{W}$ as the text from Patrice the next afternoon, along with a link.

Lydia had been folding sheets from the industrial washers and dryers that she'd installed in the laundry room. They'd been quite an expense when she'd started her business, but she still was thankful every day to have them. It meant that she could clean all the linens for the B&B, including the comforters, in a single day if she needed to.

The laundry room was warm, as always, and smelled of cotton and vinegar. While Lydia didn't have a passion for doing laundry like her mother, she did find it comforting.

The link in Patrice's text took Lydia to the Ring of Fire photography studio page. The page was dedicated to the most recent wedding that Jennifer had shot.

Lydia frowned as she started scrolling through the photos.

These did _not_ appear to be the same quality as the

work she'd seen of Jennifer's at the studio. Sure, there was her ring of fire technique, but even that couldn't hide the fact that pictures were blurry or off-center.

The composition of the group shot looked wrong to her. It took her a minute to realize that the groomsmen had been arranged wrong. She would have swapped the taller one for one of the shorter ones, made him stand at the back.

What was going on?

The bride had gone through the pictures, only liking them, giving some a thumbs up, not leaving hearts by all of them.

These weren't the work of the consummate professional who Lydia had spoken with the day before. Then again, that professional hadn't been there the entire time, either.

Had Jennifer just been having an off day? Had she been so shaken by her husband's death that she was putting up the worst of the pictures? Or were these actually the work of someone else?

If Jennifer hadn't been at the wedding, taking photographs, but someone else had been…That would destroy Jennifer's alibi. But who had she gotten to take the photos for her?

However, just a bad photoshoot wasn't evidence, at least nothing that would hold up in court. Lydia needed something else to go on.

At this point, she wouldn't even bother Ellis with her suspicions. They weren't talking about the case. Or about much of anything, really.

Lydia texted Patrice back, agreeing that something was

wrong with the pictures.

Just as Lydia had picked up the next pillowcase to fold, another text came. This one was from Misty, telling Lydia to check her email.

With a sigh, Lydia put down the warm pillowcase and looked at her inbox.

There was an official notice from the Yakima police department, telling her that the Cornflower room had been released and that the next of kin had been contacted about picking up Ricky's belongings.

Fortunately, following that was an email from Jennifer, at Ring of Fire photography, telling her to just box up Ricky's things that were in the hotel room and mail them to her, with an address. Evidently, Jennifer had already had someone ready to come down and pick up Ricky's van, with all the musical equipment in the back.

That seemed…odd. It made sense that she'd arranged to have the van picked up. Why not stick around though, or come back down, for his suitcase and belongings? It wasn't because viewing her dead husband's belongings would be too painful. No, Lydia had pegged Jennifer as too much of a control freak to allow anyone else to handle it.

Stranger and stranger.

The good news was that Lydia didn't have to scramble to find a room for the guests scheduled to arrive tomorrow who were supposed to be staying in that room.

Lydia debated for a moment, then she decided she really wanted to get those wet towels off the floor of the Cornflower room and start turning it over.

She hurried up the stairs to the third floor.

Huh. The tape across the doorway to the Cornflower room had fallen. Lydia walked up to it slowly. Had someone been up here? The tape was down on the side closest to the lock.

She picked up the end of the blue painter's tape and stuck it back to the door jamb. It stayed there for a moment, then fluttered back down.

Painter's tape would hold for a long time the first time it was stuck to something. If you peeled it off and tried to restick it, it might or might not hold.

Had someone been in the room? Lydia was going to have to check the spare key downstairs, to make sure it was still there.

Lydia unlocked the door but didn't immediately open it. She told herself that no one was waiting just inside the door to jump out at her. Still, she paused, waiting for a few moments before she pushed the door open, her hands trembling just a little bit.

She breathed a huge sigh of relief when she realized the room, indeed, did appear pretty much exactly as she'd seen it on Saturday.

It was only after Lydia stepped across the threshold that she realized something was different.

It wasn't the contents of the room. No, the bed was still unmade with the sheets all crumpled up at the foot of it. The suitcase still lay open on the desk, its belongings spilling out. A candle still stood on the desk, under the TV. Even the towels at the foot of the bed, (yes, ewww, wet), were still there.

No, the room *smelled* different.

It took Lydia a few moments to identify the sweet

scent.

Patchouli.

The perfume that Jennifer wore.

Lydia now remembered the morning when Ricky had called her into his room, saying that something smelled funny.

Had Jennifer been there? Both times?

Lydia looked around in frustration. Should she touch anything? If she tried to tell Detective Blowhard, he'd take his own sweet time coming out to Lake Hope, insisting that she leave the room as it was until he got there. She had guests coming! And besides, what was there to see? If there'd been anything incriminating left behind in the B&B room, Jennifer (or whoever) would have surely taken it by now.

Still, Lydia felt obligated to tell someone. She dragged out her phone and reluctantly called Ellis.

"Hi there," Ellis answered, cheerily. "How are you?"

"Good," Lydia said with a sigh.

"But? I feel there's a huge 'but' after that," Ellis said.

"No wonder you're a detective," Lydia snarked. "I, uhm, I got the room released back to me. Richard Hollingsworth's room. I just came up here to clean it."

"Is there something wrong with the room, ma'am?" Ellis said.

Lydia deflated as she stood there, swaying suddenly to one side, as if she no longer had the strength to stand up anymore.

The cop had come back. Not her boyfriend, Ellis. Though honestly, what had she expected? Particularly if she had news about the case?

"I can't tell if someone's been through here, searching for something or not," Lydia said. "Everything appears to be in the right place."

"Then why are you calling me?" Ellis asked. He started to sound angry.

"There's a smell in the room. Patchouli. It was here before, once, when Ricky was staying here," Lydia said. She knew it sounded ridiculous. If only she could somehow signal that she needed to talk to Ellis, not Detective Avery!

"A smell," Ellis said. He sounded doubtful.

Lydia hesitated, but decided to tell him anyway. "It's the same scent that his wife, Jennifer uses. But as far as I know, she's never been in here, in the B&B or in the room." Though Lydia still thought Jennifer looked familiar.

"Could it be the smell of the perfume from the guest staying below the room?" Ellis asked reasonably.

"Yes, it could be. I know, I know. Leaky old building. The smell could be coming from anywhere. But—I wouldn't call you if I thought it was nothing," Lydia said hotly. "I just—I didn't want to disturb any of the poor man's belongings until I told someone about it."

"All right," Ellis said slowly. "What exactly do you expect me to do about it?"

"Tell me it's all right for me to clean his room, and mail off his suitcase to his wife," Lydia said.

"Has the room been released to you?" Ellis asked.

"Yes, it has been. I told you that already," Lydia said. "And Ricky's wife has given me instructions to mail his things to her."

"Then yes, you can go ahead and clean the room. Even if there was something there or missing, there's no good chain of evidence. It's been open and available," Ellis said.

Lydia sighed. "Okay," she said. She knew Ellis was right. The room hadn't been secured, at least not how cops thought of securing a room. Despite it being locked, anyone could have gone into it.

"I just—I just wanted to do the right thing," Lydia said after a moment.

"I know," Ellis said. "I appreciate it. But there's nothing we can do with the room at this time, except to release it."

"All right," Lydia said. "I'll let you get back to work."

"It was still good to hear from you," Ellis said.

"When will I see you again?" Lydia asked, though she knew she shouldn't.

Ellis sighed. "I don't know. We're still short-staffed."

"I'll talk with you later then," Lydia said, suddenly needing to be off the phone. "Bye!"

"Bye," Ellis said, though Lydia barely heard the word as she swiped her phone off.

Then she stood in the middle of the Cornflower room, her arms wrapped around her torso. She wasn't physically trembling, but she was shaking inside.

Someone had been here. She didn't have any proof that the police would accept. But she knew, deep in her gut, that Ricky's wife Jennifer had been in the room sometime after Saturday.

What had she found? What had she taken?

And how could Lydia prove it?

12

_____

Tuesday morning, Lydia was doing breakfast prep and still had no clue how she was going to pursue the case further. Everything seemed circumstantial: the pictures on the Ring of Fire website, the perfume scent that dissipated quickly from the Cornflower Room, and Jennifer's odd behavior. Lydia didn't have anything solid.

Maybe she was just being paranoid, though. She checked the lockbox in the laundry room that contained all the keys. The spare key for the Cornflower Room was hanging exactly where it should be. The box itself didn't appear to have been tampered with.

Misty came in before the first guests arrived, wearing a smile that could only be described as the cat with all the cream.

"What is it?" Lydia asked, pointing at Misty with her knife. "You have news. Spill."

"Who, me?" Misty said, with exaggerated innocence. "I have no idea what you're talking about!"

Lydia just growled and stared at her friend. Misty was

in all blues today: blue ribbon holding her hair back, blue top and blue shorts. But her mood was sunny.

While Lydia was in grays, a dark gray T-shirt, lighter gray shorts. She'd been tempted to put gray bobby pins to pull back her hair, but decided to go for the standard brown instead.

"So, I may have found Jennifer's ex-husband," Misty said.

Lydia paused before she sliced another wedge of grapefruit. "Why do we care about him, exactly?"

"Shows a pattern of behavior," Misty said. "You're not sure if Jennifer is capable of killing someone, right? Maybe you should ask the person who might know the most about it. Her ex."

Lydia nodded slowly. "That makes sense. Where do I find this guy?"

"He's coming here at two to meet you for coffee," Misty said gleefully.

Lydia opened her mouth, then closed it again, before she managed to say, "Thank you. What would you have done if I'd said I was through with the case, let the police handle it from now on?"

Misty snorted her derision. "I would have had someone else interview him. Then provided you with a transcript when you'd finally come to your senses."

Lydia couldn't help but giggle at that. "Thank you, my friend. You know me so well."

"That I do," Misty said. "Now, get out there and finish the upfront prep. You probably shouldn't be handling sharp objects this morning."

Lydia made a face but stepped out from behind

counter and going out into the restaurant area. She'd already started the coffee, and had gotten the tables and chairs pushed into place after she'd disinfected and cleaned everything the night before.

Sunlight came in the front windows, alighting the original wooden floor with a warm glow. The smell of coffee was overtaking the smell of the industrial chemicals she'd used the night before. All her teapots were dust free, and the rosy wallpaper behind them seemed just right. Though it was just August, she was already looking forward to running the fireplace again. This room always seemed so cozy in the wintertime.

She shook her head ruefully. She knew that the only reason she was looking forward to the winter was because she wanted everything settled again. Over the past year, her most frequent phrase was that if this had been a book she'd been reading, she already would have skipped to the last chapter.

But she didn't have time for daydreaming. There was work to be done. Work she enjoyed, no matter how much or how little effort it took.

Lydia squared her shoulders, trying to shake off her gray mood, and marched forward. She could do this, despite the uncertainty. She would carry on, because that was what she did.

---

*N*orman Fitzberger was a nervous man. He was tall, probably as tall as his ex-wife Jennifer, though she may have inched over him in heels. He was dressed in a loose-fitting short-sleeved shirt done in a light-weight off-white cotton—not quite a Mexican guayabera, though along those same lines. Ed and Alan would have given him extra points for how he wore it untucked, to hide his middle-aged paunch. His white skin looked flushed, and his dark eyes kept darting around the room, as if trying to anticipate a surprise attack. He wore his receding hair slicked back, which made him look more like a used-car salesman.

The gold cross around his neck didn't surprise Lydia. Jennifer wouldn't have married someone who wasn't loudly of the faith. Ricky had probably been a lot more religious than she'd realized. He hadn't worn a cross, but there had been that candle in his room…

Lydia got Norman some coffee and gestured for the pair of them to be seated in the middle of the room. But he'd asked instead if they could sit closer to the front window, so he could watch the street.

Really nervous.

"I suppose you want to speak to me about my ex-wife, Jennifer," Norman said after he'd mostly settled down. He didn't look at her when he spoke, but instead, kept peering out the window.

"Yes," Lydia said, grateful that Misty had made that clear as part of her invitation to Norman. "You've heard that her most recent husband was killed?"

Norman nodded as he sipped his coffee, his eyes never leaving the window. "Yes. Murdered. Probably by Jennifer."

"What?" Lydia said, surprised. She hadn't expected him to just come out and say such a thing.

So much for setting a pattern of behavior.

"My wife, my ex-wife, is not necessarily sane," Norman explained. He glanced at Lydia to see how she was taking the news. He seemed to find what he was looking for, as he continued, returning his gaze to the street. "Jennifer was, is, a delight. A free spirit. An artist, in every sense of the word. It always surprised me how well she managed to keep her business going, particularly since anything related to business was an anathema to her."

"I can see that," Lydia said, based on her own meeting with Jennifer. She had seemed like a free spirit, with her messy hair and bare feet.

"Then she got involved with this cult," Norman said with a sigh. He looked back at Lydia, his eyes solemn. "I am a God-fearing man. I believe that the Lord Jesus Christ died to save us sinners. I believe in the Virgin Mary. But there is a difference between being a Christian and belonging to a cult. I will still talk with non-Christians. Still do work with them and for them. Jennifer's cult was starting to lead her down a dark path."

He paused and gave an unconscious shiver. "She started hearing voices, and those people encouraged it. Claimed her to be some sort of prophet."

"What happened?" Lydia asked when he paused again, returning his gaze to the window. This didn't necessarily make Jennifer a suspect. Lots of people believed some crazy things.

"She accused me of infidelity," Norman said, shaking his head. "May I assure you, ma'am, that I have never been unfaithful, either in thought or in deed. But she wouldn't believe me. That cult of hers continued to feed her paranoia."

"I'm sorry," Lydia said. She wanted to believe Norman. Jennifer's third husband hadn't been as faithful. No idea about Jennifer's first husband, though.

"It was rough," Norman said, still looking out on the street. "I spent a lot of nights on my knees, asking for God's guidance."

"Did you divorce her?" Lydia asked, very curious what would actually drive two such religious people apart.

"No," Norman said. For the first time that afternoon, he smiled at her. "She presented me with divorce papers. Surprised me. I hadn't imagined that she'd had it in her. Turned out that she'd been the unfaithful one, and had already started going out with Richard Hollingsworth."

"I see," Lydia said. And she did. Quite often people would accuse others of their own guilty behavior.

She wondered, but didn't ask, if Jennifer had been unfaithful to her first husband with Norman. That seemed to be too delicate of a question. She suspected that Norman wouldn't have agreed to such behavior, may not have ended up marrying Jennifer if that had been the case.

"Have you had much contact with her since the divorce?" Lydia asked when Norman fell silent again.

"A little," Norman admitted. "I hear from both her and her sister, Holly. Jennifer still texts me, completely out of the blue. Mostly it's bible verses." He cleared his throat, took a sip of his coffee, and sat up a bit straighter, as if he had to prepare himself for what came next.

"Sunday, she sent me this," Norman said. He pulled

out his phone, then flipped it around so she could read the text.

> *Whoever conceals his transgressions*
> *will not prosper, but he who*
> *confesses and forsakes them will*
> *obtain mercy. Proverbs 28:13*

He looked at her directly. "I took it as a threat. I've never confessed to being an adulterer, because I never cheated on her, not in thought or in deed. I assume she's coming after me, to force a confession."

Lydia blinked, surprised. Why would Jennifer send such a text to her ex? That seemed out of character.

"So I'm taking a long vacation," Norman said after a few moments. "I'm driving east and south. No, I won't tell you where I'm going. I'm getting myself out of harm's way, in case Jennifer really does decide to come after me. Give her a few weeks to calm down, get over the loss of her husband."

"Do you really think that Jennifer would hunt you down?" Lydia asked. "She's an artist. That might take too much planning."

Norman nodded. "I know. I vacillate between, 'I need to go, I need to keep running,' and calling myself a fool for believing the worst of a person. And while I haven't had any direct messages from God, I still believe this is the right path, for me to get out of the way, at least for now."

Lydia suddenly understood the man's nervousness. He was afraid that Jennifer might suddenly show up like a malicious ghost, directly in his path.

"Then I won't keep you any longer," Lydia said. "Thank you so much for making time for me."

Norman gave her another smile, this time tinged with sadness. "Raul, our friend in common, said that you would be able to use your influence on the police, to get them pointed in the right direction. I believe that even if you can't get those in law enforcement to do the right thing, that you, personally, will."

"Thank you," Lydia said. Norman was right. She was going to do the right thing. It was the least she could do for her community—to bring another killer to justice.

Even if she had to do it herself.

13

_L_ater Tuesday afternoon, Lydia went over to see Patrice and to give her the latest news, to tell her about Norman and her own theories.

However, _The Palace Bakery_ was closed. Lydia texted Patrice, asking where she was, but she didn't get any response.

Worried, Lydia walked into the patio area, to the south of the building, but everything seemed fine there, all the tables and chairs stacked up and locked together with a bicycle lock.

Then she walked up the block, past the investment firm and real estate offices, then to the alley and back down, taking a look at the back of Patrice's building. She checked the door—it was locked solidly.

Patrice's car was parked in the back. There appeared to be a figure slumped over the steering wheel.

Slowly, Lydia approached. Had Jennifer gotten there first? Had she strangled Patrice with a rope, then left more heart stickers?

Lydia nearly jumped out of her skin when the figure moved. Patrice sat back, though she kept her hands wrapped firmly around the steering wheel.

Her gorgeous friend had tears streaming down her face.

Lydia froze. She didn't know if she should walk forward to comfort her friend, or if Patrice wanted to be left the hell alone.

Before Lydia could crouch down and sneak away, Patrice saw her. She appeared to take a large gulp, then nodded, pointing at the passenger door, obviously intending for Lydia to join her in the car.

Feeling guilty, Lydia slipped into the car. It was a late-model Subaru. The seats in the back were always folded down, so that Patrice had room for orders when she delivered cakes or cookies to events. The car always carried a sweet smell of sugar and candied lemon, not quite as good or as comforting as the shop, but a close second.

"I'm sorry," Lydia said as soon as she sat down. "The shop was closed and I was worried about you."

Patrice reached out and squeezed her friend's arm tightly. "I know. Thank you for caring."

Lydia placed her hand over her friend's and squeezed. "What do you need?" she asked quietly.

While Lydia had thought herself ready for anything, Patrice snatching back her hand and pounding on the steering wheel hadn't been high on her list.

"Damn those men!" Patrice said as she banged her palms again and again. "Damn them, damn them, damn them!"

Then Patrice started crying again. Lydia reached across

the center console and tried to hold onto her friend, give her some comfort.

Patrice shook her head, gently removed Lydia's hands from her shoulders, just holding onto the closest one, squeezing it tightly. Patrice's hand was hot, the palm sweaty. The rest of Patrice, despite the tears, looked as pretty as ever. Her golden, frizzy hair gently framed her face. She wore a nicer blouse and slacks, looking more dressed up than normal for a day at work.

Of course, Patrice knew how to look beautiful while crying. Her skin didn't get splotchy and her eyes didn't get bloodshot. Even though her nose was running, instead of a huge honking snort, she sniffed delicately, and that appeared to be enough to clear her system.

Lydia didn't know what had happened, but she'd rarely seen Patrice this worked up. She sat in silence, trying to exude support and comfort.

Finally, Patrice's death grip on Lydia's hand subsided and she seemed to pull herself together.

"I had deliveries to make this afternoon," Patrice said.

Lydia nodded. That explained the better outfit.

"But then that detective who's working the case, Detective Bloyer? He came into the shop and insisted that I needed to come down to the police station right away."

"Huh," Lydia said. She hadn't realized that he was back in town. Was he following Norman? Probably not. Probably had no idea that there was an ex-husband who was now in fear for his life.

"I closed up a little early, particularly when he assured me it was only going to take a few minutes." Patrice gave a weak laugh. "I should have known better, right? Should have called Gracie."

"Do you want to call Gracie now, to have her start on the deliveries?" Lydia said. "I can wait."

Patrice gave her a grateful smile and squeezed her hand again. "Yes. Thank you." She pulled out her phone and grimaced. "Text from you worrying about me?" she asked.

"Duh," Lydia said.

Patrice merely nodded, then called Gracie and asked if she could make the deliveries that afternoon. Evidently she could, and Lydia could tell that made Patrice relax even further.

"Anyway, that detective got me into one of the back interview rooms at the station, then started barraging me with questions about where I'd been on Friday, why had I had my phone turned off, and so on." Patrice gave a delicate shudder. "At least Sergeant Gonzales was there, to play good cop."

Lydia bit her lips together so she didn't say anything. Detective Blowhard must have been pretty bad if Sergeant Gonzales was the "good" cop.

"You weren't at the bakery?" Lydia asked, surprised. Generally, Patrice was at the bakery as much as Lydia was at the B&B.

"No," Patrice said with a sad shake of her head. "I'd arranged with Gracie to be at the store all Friday so I could make deliveries and get home early. Dan was going to be there, and I hadn't seen him in a week."

Lydia nodded. "What happened to your phone?"

"I'd rebooted the stupid thing," Patrice said. "Or at least I'd thought I had. Seemed I'd powered it all the way off instead of restarting it. Didn't realize it until much later, after I was home."

"Ouch," Lydia said.

Patrice shrugged. "I figured it was fine, as I hadn't missed any important calls or texts. But the detective found it highly suspicious. And then both he and the sergeant started haranguing me about the restraining order. They were treating me as if it had been my fault, as if I'd been encouraging Mr. Hollingsworth."

Patrice gripped the steering wheel hard again, her knuckles turning white. "I did *not* encourage that man. I never would do something like that."

"But when they'd interviewed Jennifer Hollingsworth, that would be exactly the sort of thing that she'd accuse you of," Lydia said.

Patrice stared hard at Lydia.

Lydia could hear the word that Patrice used in her head, but never said out loud.

"I didn't. I swear to you. I didn't," Patrice said.

"I know you didn't," Lydia said, reaching across the center of the seat, wrapping her fingers gently around Patrice's wrist and squeezing. "They're just being assholes."

"You got that right," Patrice said. She leaned back, dropping her hands, and Lydia drew her own hand back. "I'm as much pissed off as worried. I have no alibi. They think I'm a great candidate for killing Mr. Hollingsworth."

"But you didn't," Lydia said. "Probably his wife did."

"How do we prove that?" Patrice said, her voice rising again. "Particularly if the police aren't going to listen to me? To us?"

"Well, we suspect Jennifer didn't take those pictures at

that wedding, right?" Lydia said after a few moments. "We're going to have to figure out who did."

She told Patrice about her interview with Norman, and how he was now in fear for his life. Just before he'd left he'd assured her that if it was God's plan for him to die, he would go with grace. However, that didn't mean lying down on the road waiting for a car to drive over him.

"So the ex-husband thinks she did it, and that he's next. Wonder what the first husband thinks?" Patrice mused.

"Misty hasn't been able to get in contact with the first husband. He also appears to have disappeared off the face of the earth," Lydia said with a grimace.

"Who are Jennifer's friends?" Patrice said. "Do you think it was someone else in her cult?"

"I doubt any of them would confess to it, if that was the case," Lydia said. Then she paused for a moment, thinking. "Wait. Norman mentioned that Jennifer had a sister. Holly. Could she have been the one at the wedding, taking pictures? While Jennifer went to the vineyard and killed her husband?"

"It's possible," Patrice said slowly. "But how did Jennifer know that Mr. Hollingsworth was going to be at the vineyard? On the tour?"

"That would be in either his phone texts or in his emails," Lydia said. "And we don't have access to those. We just have to assume that he told his wife where he was going. She's the jealous type. He may have felt that he needed to keep her informed of his whereabouts all the damned time."

Patrice nodded. "We need to find that sister. And

soon. Before that detective just decides to lock me up on suspicion."

"We won't let that happen," Lydia said firmly. "I'll set Misty on it."

"Thank you," Patrice said. She gave Lydia a real smile for the first time that afternoon. "It's good to know that you have friends who have your back."

"Absolutely," Lydia said. "We'll solve this. Before they do."

Because now it wasn't just about bringing a murderer to justice, but also about protecting her best friend.

14

_____

*A*fter Lydia left Patrice with a promise to call her later that evening, she walked back along Main Street, before turning and going to the post office. She thought fondly of the older buildings the post office had inhabited before moving to this new, modern, purpose-built building.

Plexiglass still hung between the postal workers and their customers. However, masks were no longer required inside the building. The postal workers still wore them, though.

Lydia checked her post office box. Of course, there were the usual brochures for political candidates. Though it was an off year and no major elections were happening, there were a few minor ones being contested.

Such as the Judiciary Advisory Committee.

Lydia gulped when she saw the postcard from Alan Turflow. It claimed that you should vote for an upstanding member of the community, one who was more in line with the conservative values of the community.

What was he implying by that? Lydia tossed it into the recycle bin. She was heading toward the door when she heard someone call out, "Lydia?"

"Hey," Lydia said, turning to find her mom there, carrying an empty bag. "Just dropping off your own brochures?" she teased.

Mom nodded, but she didn't look pleased. She was still in what Ed and Alan would call dressed-up office wear, with a nice amber blouse, a short khaki skirt, and comfortable flats. She had golden hoop earrings that Lydia hadn't seen before, but they looked pretty.

"I did," Mom said absentmindedly. Then she thrust one of Alan Turflow's brochures at Lydia. "Did you see this trash?"

"Yeah," Lydia said as she held the door open for her mom. "What is he talking about?"

"Your brother, I would imagine," Mom said, sounding displeased.

"What would Theo—Oh," Lydia said, putting it together.

"This is a more conservative area," Mom admitted. She slipped her hand into the crook of Lydia's arm.

Lydia took the hint and bent her elbow so it was more comfortable as she and her mom walked outside. The sky was that brilliant blue that you only got toward the end of summer, with no clouds to be seen. The smell of baking concrete filled the air. It was hot outside, but not beastly so. They still stuck to the shaded side of the street, which was noticeably cooler.

It would only be a month or so before fall would start

shadowing their doorsteps, demure at first before gustily blowing the leaves around and heralding the rain.

"I don't know if you heard, but during the debate Alan wondered out loud how I would be able to advise the Judicial Board about family matters when my own family was so tainted?"

"He really said that?" Lydia said, aghast. Theo might be many things, but tainted?

"Yes, he did," Mom said.

Lydia could tell that her mother was still angry about it. Where did this Alan guy get off, talking trash about her family?

"I had really thought I'd be able to do some good by running," Mom said in a low voice. "I hadn't thought that people would be dragging my family into it."

"You aren't thinking about backing out, are you?" Lydia said.

Her mom pressed her lips together and didn't say anything.

That wasn't good enough.

Lydia stopped them in the middle of the sidewalk. The tourists following behind them nearly plowed into them, but managed to swerve around them at the last moment. Lydia pulled them over to one of the convenient benches that lined the street, sitting down abruptly and dragging her mother down with her.

"Look, Mom, if you decide you're not having fun, that's one thing. But you can't quit just because someone's being a bully. Theo can stand up for himself." She gave a quiet snort. "Theo would actually *love* the chance to stand up for himself. He'd gladly come to any event you named, with Steven, and would proudly stand up on the stage with you."

"I know," Mom sighed. She patted Lydia's arm. "I do know. And I know that I shouldn't expect a weasel like Alan Turflow to go easy on me because it's my first time running for office. I just thought it would be different, you know?"

Lydia shook her head. "Nope. Don't know. I didn't expect anything different. In fact, I bet it's been easy for now, and that it's just going to getting nastier."

"Okay," Mom said slowly.

"There's going to be a lot of gossip about you and Dad," Lydia said. "A lot. You know how small towns are."

"You're right," Mom said, nodding.

"Luckily, you've got good friends, people you can rely on to tell you the truth, who won't lie to you about what's being said, or what you should say," Lydia continued. "Like Jen McGowen."

"True," Mom said. "I hadn't thought of that."

Lydia rolled her eyes. "You've been doing everything all by yourself, haven't you?" She'd always known that her parents worked hard. She should have realized before that a control freak like her mother wouldn't hand off anything.

"I can't afford to pay anyone, not really," Mom said defensively.

"That's why they're called volunteers," Lydia pointed out.

"You're right, I know you're right," Mom said. "But I just have problems asking people to help."

"I know," Lydia said. "I inherited that from you. So

how about this? I will ask Jen McGowen for you, to see if she can find some time to volunteer for your campaign. Then, I need you to do something for me."

Mom gave her a sly smile. "Is this what they meant by campaign promises and favors?"

"Possibly," Lydia said.

After a moment, Mom prompted Lydia with, "What is it that you want?"

Lydia sighed. She didn't want to tell her mom all about the murder that she was currently trying to solve. "How would you go about finding a missing, deadbeat husband?" she asked.

"So I could possibly garnish his wages?" Mom said. "I'd start with the DMV. See if he still has a driver's license."

"Are DMV records public?" Lydia asked, surprised.

"They are in Washington State," Mom assured her. "What, did a client skip out of the B&B without paying you?"

Lydia tilted her head from side to side. "Something like that." It might be a start for how to find Jennifer's first husband.

"Thank you," Mom said as she and Lydia stood back up. "I didn't realize how much I needed some help."

"You're welcome," Lydia said, squeezing the hand that was tucked back into her elbow again. "Your family will stand behind you, no matter what choices you make. You know that, right?"

"Well, sure, as long as it doesn't involve putting my fliers in her restaurant," Mom teased.

Lydia thought for a moment. "I will, though. Just to prove to that asshole that we aren't afraid of him."

"No," Mom said, shaking her head. "As you said, you'll end up alienating half the town by taking sides."

"But you're my mother," Lydia pointed out gently. "That means I've already taken sides. And if people don't know that, too bad."

"Are you sure?" Mom asked as they reached her car in the parking lot beside the post office.

"Positive," Lydia said.

Mom picked up a handful of brochures from a box in the back seat of the car. Lydia took them from her before she could change her mind.

"It'll be fine," she assured her mother, and herself.

They promised to see each other soon, and Lydia took off down the street, heading to the B&B.

She really didn't want to alienate half the town by actively campaigning for her mother. However, if Alan Turflow was really going to be an idiot and attack her family, well, he deserved what he got.

Not that she'd purposefully go digging up dirt on him. She might, though, ask Misty if she knew anything. Just as a matter of research...

15

*L*ater that evening, Lydia retired to her rooms with a well-earned glass of wine. She was curled up on the loveseat that night, reading a true-crime book, written by the wife of a serial killer.

She kept shaking her head at the poor woman. Given the wife's upbringing she didn't stand a chance figuring out that there was something wrong with her "prince." He was actually normal given what she'd been raised with.

It felt good to be ensconced, safe in her rooms, reading about other people's troubles. Her own list of worries was getting longer—finding Jennifer Hollingsworth's sister, to see if she knew anything about Ricky's murder; fighting back against Alan Turflow and his smear campaign against the Marsh family; and then figuring out her own troubles with Ellis.

As if on cue, her phone rang. With a sigh, Lydia put down her book and picked it up.

It was Ellis.

"Hi there," Lydia said, trying to make herself at least sound cheerful.

"What's up?" Ellis asked. She could see him in his apartment in Yakima, the lights dimmed, sitting in his recliner, a beer gathering drops of condensation on the end table beside him.

"Just the usual," Lydia said. "Alan Turflow is being a turd to my mom, trying to use Theo to smear our family as well as her campaign. The police think that Patrice killed Ricky, which you and I both know is ridiculous. And—"

"I really can't talk about the case with you," Ellis said tersely.

"I know," Lydia said. "But I need to be able to talk with someone about it. We're pretty sure that Jennifer, Ricky's wife, did it. I just need to figure out how she got out of the wedding shoot she was supposedly in. If she was there at all."

Ellis sighed. "We're not having this conversation."

"Did you know that Jennifer's second husband is in fear for his life? That he's so convinced that now that Jennifer's killed her third husband, she's coming after him next?" Lydia said. She found that she not only was standing, but was pacing across her small living floor.

"No," Ellis said. "And I can't know those things either. You're prejudicing me against the case."

"But you aren't working the case, are you?" Lydia said. "Joe Blowhard is the detective in charge."

"Detective Bloyer is the person in charge," Ellis said.

It sounded as if he was talking through gritted teeth.

"He made Patrice cry," Lydia said. "Asking her questions and then never listening to her answers."

"I'm sure he had his reasons for treating a potential suspect that way," Ellis said.

"He was so bad that Sergeant Gonzales was reduced to playing good cop," Lydia said. She couldn't help but snort with derision. "You know it has to be bad if the sergeant needs to resort to that."

"Can we please talk about something else? Anything else?" Ellis said, practically begging.

"Sure," Lydia said. "What are we doing? Where are we going with this relationship? It's been about a year."

Stunned silence greeted her, before Ellis finally said, "I, ah, I thought we were having fun."

Lydia shook her head. She knew she shouldn't be springing this on him out of the blue.

Or was it out of the blue? She wasn't sure. That was a big part of the problem. She was never certain where she stood with Ellis.

"Is it just fun? There's nothing more serious going on between us?" Lydia said after a moment.

She found herself standing in the middle of her living room with her arms wrapped around herself, as if the cool of the evening had somehow snuck inside.

This was far too familiar of a position, as far as she was concerned. Hugging herself because there was no one here who she could hold onto.

Ellis sighed. "I thought we were having fun. Is this no longer fun for you?"

Lydia shook her head. "It's been fun. But were you aware that our one-year anniversary is next week?"

"No?" Ellis said, sounding timid. "I don't really keep track of those sorts of things."

Lydia nodded. It was such a guy thing, putting all the emotional work on the female in the relationship.

It was just one more thing that she didn't like about their relationship.

"It's just, a year's time, it's kind of a marker, you know?" Lydia said. She didn't want to come out and say what was on her mind, now that the moment was here, staring her in the face.

"I see," Ellis said. "It's a time for reflection, and for planning, right?"

"Exactly," Lydia said. A small bud of hope spang up. The flower hadn't opened yet, but maybe there was a chance.

"What if I tell you I'm happy with how things are, and I don't see any changes in the near future?" Ellis said.

"What about the not so near future?" Lydia asked.

"I don't know," Ellis said truthfully.

Lydia nodded. "If you don't know after a year's time, will you know after two years' time? Three?"

"You know that isn't fair," Ellis said. "I don't know how I'll feel. Where you'll be. Where I'll be."

"I'll still be here in Lake Hope," Lydia pointed out. "I'm not about to move anywhere. And you'll still be in Yakima, unless you get a promotion-slash-transfer to a bigger city. Like Seattle."

The heavy sigh that Ellis gave felt as if it carried the weight of the world. "I guess what you're asking is to either fish or cut bait," he said eventually.

"I think we might be to that point, yeah," Lydia said.

"My mom asked me if the good times were enough to get us through the bad times. And I just haven't been sure, you know?"

"I hadn't realized we were having any bad times," Ellis said.

Lydia nearly rolled her eyes. "It's the whole 'cop' thing."

"Oh. Yeah. That," Ellis said. He paused, then said, "If it wasn't for the current case, and your best friend being involved, would we still be here? Or is it just what's going on now?"

Lydia had to think about that for a moment before she finally replied, "Yes, we would be. It might not be now, at the one-year anniversary. It might have been the two year instead. But I think...I think...yes. We would still probably get to this point sooner or later."

"I see," Ellis said.

The hard quality of his voice told Lydia that he didn't understand, not really.

"Then I guess this is goodbye, at least for now," Ellis said abruptly.

Lydia blinked, a little taken aback. But Ellis had always been a "pull the bandage off quickly" kind of guy.

"I guess you're right," she said softly. "I do still care for you. But I think it's probably for the best."

"I'll mail you your things," Ellis said.

"And I'll do the same," Lydia said, though there was so little of Ellis in her rooms.

And possibly that was part of the problem. They'd never let each other fully in.

"Goodbye," Ellis said softly. "Good luck. Stay safe."

"Goodbye," Lydia said. "Same to you."

She swiped off her phone. The weight of everything suddenly came crashing down on her and she collapsed onto her loveseat.

A few tears leaked out of her eyes, leaving cold tracks down her cheeks. However, she found she didn't need to cry much more than that.

She wouldn't admit it to anyone, not until much later, but instead of sadness, all she felt was a sense of relief.

16

*W*ednesday morning, Lydia found herself alternating between feeling happy and feeling sad. She couldn't stay too long in either position, though. She would take a sip of her coffee and would sigh happily because it was absolutely perfect that morning. Then she'd think about how she should tell Ellis about her delightful morning, and would grow sad again.

She honestly wasn't sad about losing the relationship. If she was being honest with herself, it had been going bad for a while. No, she was more upset about losing the potential. They could have been great. They would never have that chance, now.

However, she wasn't hiding anything from Misty. Even if she'd wanted to, Misty took one look at her and immediately asked, "What's wrong?"

"I, uhm, I broke up with Ellis last night," Lydia said. The words were actually really difficult, as if saying it out loud made it more real. Plus, technically, Ellis had been the one to break it off with her.

"Oh, honey, I'm sorry," Misty said. She narrowed her eyes at Lydia. "Is there brandy in that coffee? You seem awfully happy with it."

"What? No!" Lydia said. She held out the mug for Misty to sniff. "It's just really good coffee this morning."

"I see," Misty said. She paused, crossing her arms over her chest and looking up at Lydia. Misty was wearing a cute pink blouse that morning, with just a touch of lace at the collar and on the breast pockets. "If I didn't know better, I'd say you weren't crying too much over this breakup."

Lydia shrugged. She knew she wasn't acting how everyone else probably thought she should be acting. She wasn't sure how she should be feeling, quite frankly.

"It's all right," Misty said, nodding. "I just want you to be happy. And while Ellis made you happy sometimes, there were too many times when he didn't."

Lydia felt herself breaking into a huge smile at that. "You're right, he didn't." She put her coffee down and started pacing. "What would make me happy is to find Jennifer's sister. See if she knows who might have taken the pictures at the wedding. It couldn't have been Jennifer."

"Jennifer's sister's name is Holly Pensworth," Misty said. "But I'm still having problems tracking down where she's currently staying. She was living with Jennifer and Ricky when they were in Spokane. Her mail is coming to a post office box there."

"Do I need to make a trip to Spokane? To haunt her mailbox?" Lydia asked, only somewhat kidding.

Misty shrugged. "Possibly. Or maybe go to Benson, see if you can find her there."

"What does she look like?" Lydia said. "Do you have a recent photo of her?"

"No," Misty said. "She has a bunny icon that she uses online, not a picture of herself."

"So we just need to find a woman who likes rabbits," Lydia joked.

"She might have a purse that has bunnies on it," Misty said seriously. "Or maybe a bumper sticker on her car. Don't you worry. I have people out and looking for her."

That was only slightly reassuring for Lydia. She really didn't want to know what sorts of resources Misty had called into play. Particularly since Lydia had told her about Patrice, and how the cops appeared to think she might be guilty.

Misty wasn't merely protective of Lydia, but of her whole town. Lydia remembered one time when she had teased Misty, calling her the Grandmother Mafia.

Misty had taken that personally, warning Lydia off the name.

Maybe there was such a thing. Who knew.

Lydia fell back into her normal routine for the rest of the day, working in the restaurant in the morning and during lunch, then changing over rooms in the afternoon.

It wasn't until later on that evening that she started getting lonely. She wasn't going to get a call from Ellis. Not that she would have been expecting one, even if they hadn't broken up. No, he never called two nights in a row.

Honestly, she never knew when he call. Which part of the problem.

She spent part of that evening thinking about what she actually wanted in a partner. Someone who could be there in half an hour, not an hour and a half. Someone she could depend on. Someone who would tell her about his day, and not censor out almost all of the things he'd done. Someone who would be interested in what she'd done, would either be able to talk about the hotel and restaurant business, or be willing to learn.

She fell asleep in her cozy bedroom with the window opened slightly to let in the cool night air, and woke up refreshed.

She found she barely thought about Ellis the next day. Though it had been less than forty-eight hours, it already felt like forty-eight weeks ago.

She took that as another sign that she'd done the right thing.

Just as Lydia was finishing up bussing all the lunch dishes back to the kitchen to be cleaned, Misty called her.

"A Holly Pensworth just signed in at the Greenwood Hair Salon," Misty said as a way of greeting.

"Really?" Lydia said, surprised. "I guess I may need to get my own hair cut."

"Wash that man right out of your hair," Misty said. Lydia could hear the grin in her voice.

It was the typical response to a breakup—for a woman to cut her hair.

Lydia wasn't about to chop off her hair. She actually really liked it. When it was up, she could pull it back from her face and off her neck. When it was down, which was how she wore it during the winter, it was a lovely extra layer of warmth on her back.

But she could see about getting it trimmed…

Misty said she'd be back to the B&B in a short while and would work with Alice on changing over the two rooms that guests had checked out of.

In the meanwhile, Lydia had someone she had to go interview.

17

*L*ydia found herself squinting at the harsh scent of the chemicals in the salon. Ugh. She couldn't stay there. The smell hadn't brought tears to her eyes, but it was pretty bad.

The salon was tiny, with a small receptionist's desk to the right of the door. A tall screen blocked the view of the rest of the shop. The screen had a gorgeous painting of a golden moon with a crane standing on one leg in front of it. Soft pop music played, though Lydia remembered that the other times she'd come in here, they'd been playing country.

Beyond the screen, on the same wall as the desk, were three chairs in front of three mirrors. Past that were two sinks for washing hair, a restroom, and a huge supply closet filled with shampoo, extra gowns, and every color of dye a client might need.

A young woman with blue hair stood behind the receptionist's desk. She smiled cheerily at Lydia. "Hi! Do you have an appointment?"

"No, I don't," Lydia said after a moment. "I'm actually here to pick up a friend. Holly?"

"She's still getting her hair cut. You can wait there," the receptionist said, indicating the three chairs that were against the wall, opposite the desk. Lurid magazines were piled up on a table between them.

Lydia took a moment to peer beyond the screen. Luckily, only one chair was occupied. Lydia couldn't really get a good look at the woman seated there, as she was facing away from the mirror, her eyes closed, with the stylist trimming her bangs.

"I think I'll wait outside," Lydia said. She felt as though her lungs were under attack. They really needed a much better ventilation system in such a tiny space!

"Okay!" the young woman said cheerfully before going back to her own magazine.

Lydia took a deep breath once she stood outside. There was a reason why she trimmed her own hair. Going regularly to a salon was far too expensive, plus she couldn't stand the smell.

While it might be fun to think about getting her hair cut short, Lydia had tried it a couple of times and hated it every time. She liked having long hair, and didn't see herself changing her hair style anytime soon.

Particularly not just because she'd broken up with her boyfriend.

What was she going to say to Holly? How could she just go walking up to her and accuse her sister of killing her husband? She had to think of something, and quick.

At least the salon was on the shady side of the street. Lydia paced, coming up with one excuse after another.

Did she pretend she wanted to interview Holly about her experience at the salon? Or ask her about her sister and her photography? She'd claimed to be a friend, but she knew nothing about Holly.

Damn it! She wished she was more prepared.

Before she could work herself up more, Holly came walking out the salon door.

Lydia didn't have a chance to think about anything. She said the first thing that came to her mind.

"Jennifer? Jennifer Hollingsworth?" Lydia said as she walked forward.

Holly didn't look exactly like her sister. They were close enough, though, that they could use the same driver's license. Holly, like Jennifer, was about as tall as Lydia, thin, and cute. She had longish sandy-blonde hair that hung down to just past her shoulders. Her bangs framed wide gray-green eyes that looked a little lost. She wore a loose white-and-red tie-dyed shirt and a pair of beige shorts that also looked a little big on her.

A large black camera hung from her neck, and she carried a black bag that looked as though it held more camera gear.

"Uhm, yes?" Holly said.

Lydia was a bit taken back. She knew that the person standing in front of her wasn't Jennifer. Jennifer was a lot skinnier. Plus, though Lydia didn't know Jennifer very well, she was certain that the photographer would never go anywhere without her gold cross.

However, Lydia decided to play along with Holly's game, to see if she could trip the other woman up.

"Lydia Marsh," Lydia said, introducing herself. "I

drove up to Benson to see you last week, to talk about possibly shooting my wedding."

"Right," Holly said, nodding. Her smile stayed tentative.

"Can I buy you a cup of coffee? Talk a bit more about my plans?" Lydia asked, trying to keep her own smile innocent and friendly.

Why was Holly impersonating her sister? Did they do this regularly?

"I'm sorry, I'm on my way to check out a location for a shoot," Holly said, trying to gracefully get out of the conversation.

"Are you really? Jennifer?" Lydia said. She reached out and grabbed hold of Holly's wrist. "Or are you just trying to not get caught out, *Holly*?"

The woman in front of her froze. She would have bolted had Lydia not been holding on to her.

"What do you mean?" Holly said, her voice breaking.

"Do you want to go get some coffee, Holly?" Lydia said. She kept her hand wrapped tightly around the other woman's wrist. Holly's face started turning red. "Maybe over at *The Palace Bakery*?"

Lydia suddenly remembered where she'd seen Jennifer, or rather, Holly, before. She'd been at Patrice's bakery, ordering some gluten-free goodies.

While the two points of Holly's cheeks stayed a bright red, the rest of her face suddenly turned ashen. "Who are you?" Holly said, barely whispering. "Did…did my sister send you?"

"No, Jennifer didn't send me," Lydia said. "I know

you're not Jennifer. You're her sister, Holly. Why? Why would you think she'd sent me?" She suddenly put two and two together and really didn't like the four that she came up with. "Did Jennifer threaten you?"

Holly didn't reply. But the gulp she gave said volumes.

"It's all right," Lydia said, suddenly speaking more softly, trying to console the other woman. "I won't let Jennifer near you. You'll be safe."

Holly shook her head. "I don't know," she said.

Her hand was trembling.

"Let's go talk, quietly, by ourselves," Lydia said. "I know the local police. We can keep you safe." She'd pull on her big girl britches and call Ellis if she had to. Or even Detective Bloyer.

Holly looked up and down the street, as if she was afraid Jennifer might suddenly show up. It reminded Lydia of Norman, how he kept looking around for Jennifer.

"Where do you want to go to talk?" Lydia asked, stepping closer into Holly's space.

"Not *The Palace*," Holly said firmly. "Jennifer's kind of obsessed with that place."

"Gotcha," Lydia said. She was going to have to let Patrice know. "I own a B&B nearby. Want to come and talk with me there?"

"All right," Holly said.

Lydia turned and started walking back down Main Street toward the B&B, finally letting go of Holly's arm when the other woman started walking beside her.

"I went to the salon to get my hair all cut off," Holly said after a few moments. "I was going to change it completely so that Jennifer and I would no longer look anything alike. But Jennifer told me that accidents happened to those who didn't obey the word of the Lord. So I kept it long, exactly like hers."

"How long have you been impersonating each other?" Lydia asked, hoping to get onto less emotionally trying ground.

"Since we were kids," Holly told her with a grin. She finally appeared to be breathing normally, and her face had regained its normal color. "Jennifer's only two years older than me. And we were born just a few days apart. She was born on the twenty-first of March, while I was born on the twenty-fifth."

"That must have been fun, back then," Lydia said. She and Theo had never had a great relationship, but she knew other people actually liked their siblings. Or at least had grown to like them once they'd become adults, as she and Theo had.

"It was." Holly turned more sober. "That was before Jennifer found religion."

They'd reached the B&B at that point. Lydia opened the door and issued Holly in. She got coffee for both of them, as well as some of the gluten-free cookies that she'd bought from Patrice the day before. She arranged them on a platter because that was one of the things she did regularly, adding beauty to everyday events.

Ed and Alan would have been proud. Possibly even Poe wouldn't have turned up his nose.

It took Lydia a moment to realize that Ellis would never have noticed the effort she'd gone to. And how sad was that?

Holly seemed absorbed in her coffee, sitting at a table in the middle of the empty restaurant. She had both hands wrapped around her mug and looked deeply into it, as if seeking out the answers to all the mysteries in the world.

"Here," Lydia said, putting the plate on the table, then turning it just so, presenting it to Holly.

"Wow," Holly said. "Mind if I take a picture of that?"

"Sure, go ahead," Lydia said. It wasn't anything special. She had put the cookies on a pretty summer platter, that had beautiful purple plums along the edges, bright yellow flowers in the center, and all tied together with leaves that were colored from blue to green. The half dozen cookies were in a neat row in the center, a golden brown. They were Lydia's favorite, a type of "shortbread" that was made from almond flour, hazelnuts, and rosemary—no actual butter was involved.

Lydia sat with her own coffee, watching Holly. She seemed fairly familiar with her camera, quickly taking a dozen shots before she sat back, suddenly exhausted. She took the camera strap from around her neck and placed the equipment on the table.

While Holly had been busy taking her pictures, Lydia had picked up her cellphone and put it on the table as well. She'd set it to record their conversation, in case Holly got cold feet.

Even if the recording couldn't be used in court, because Lydia hadn't asked permission to record the conversation, at least it would give the detectives something to go on.

"What was it like growing up with Jennifer?" Lydia asked, trying to feel her way back into their discussion.

"You know how the eldest child is generally the responsible one? Not Jennifer. She was wild. I felt like I was the older sibling sometimes," Holly said. She picked up one of the cookies, nibbled on it, then sighed before she resumed speaking. "I never drank while I was in high school. Not really. Jennifer did. And she smoked pot. I'm pretty sure she did other drugs when I wasn't there, like cocaine and heroin." Holly shuddered. "I wouldn't touch those sorts of things. Too great a chance that I'd get hooked for life, you know?"

"I do," Lydia said. There had been some wild kids at her high school, back in the day. She'd never been tempted to fall into that crowd. She'd been one of the smart kids, taking AP classes, destined for college, at the time, looking to leave Lake Hope and never come back.

"Jennifer stopped drinking and doing drugs in her mid-twenties. She was in AA for a long while, but then she found this cult, which told her that all she needed was the Virgin Mary," Holly said with a grimace. "Jennifer's always been an addict, I guess. She's replaced one addiction for another."

"How did she meet Ricky?" Lydia said, trying to direct the conversation.

"He was actually part of the same cult," Holly said with a laugh tinged with bitterness. "Although, I don't think he was a true believer. As most of the people in the cult were women, I think he just joined in order to have his pick of the lot."

"That sounds a lot like Ricky," Lydia said dryly, given what she knew of him.

"He was kind of creepy," Holly said, leaning forward a bit, as if sharing a secret.

"He was, wasn't he," Lydia said, mirroring her action.

"While Jennifer was an addict, Ricky was just obsessive. He'd get interested in something, go all in for a while, before turning around and deciding he didn't care about it in the least." Holly shook her head. "I think he was that way about Jennifer, to be quite honest. He was fascinated by her, decided to marry her, then, when his interest faded, he started looking around at other women."

"Was he unfaithful to her?" Lydia said, curious.

"I think so," Holly said. "I mean, I could believe him when he said he was innocent, or I could believe my sister, you know? That was a pretty easy choice."

"And her previous husbands?" Lydia said.

Holly shrugged. "Again, who do I believe? This man who I've only known for a few years? Or my sister, who I've known all my life?"

"So what happened with Ricky?" Lydia said.

Holly put her coffee mug on the table. She appeared to collapse, her shoulders drooping. "I don't know," she said quietly, her voice breaking.

"Something happened to him," Lydia said. "Someone killed him."

"I know," Holly said, her eyes still trained on her coffee mug, not looking up at Lydia. "I don't want to think that it was Jennifer. She's my sister, you know?"

Lydia let the moment of silence between them stretch. She could feel that Holly wanted to say something more.

Finally, Holly looked up. She looked sad, but more determined than she had before.

"I don't know if Jennifer killed Ricky. What I do know is that she has no alibi."

"You were the one who took the pictures at the wedding, weren't you?" Lydia asked quietly.

"I was."

18

Holly appeared to fall apart after making her confession. She started crying, and it took Lydia a while before she could finally get the other woman to calm down.

"Taking the pictures for Jennifer, that wasn't the worst part," Holly said as she dried her eyes with a napkin. "The worst part was having her scream at me about how awful the shots were."

"I'm sorry," Lydia said, though she agreed that most of those shots had been pretty bad. "What happened?"

"I brought the wrong gear," Holly said. "And…I don't *do* people. That's not my thing. I take pictures of nature. Of buildings. Of cars. I can take amazing pictures of a stream or even a plate of cookies." She gave Lydia a watery grin. "But I don't like dealing with people."

"Do you still have the shots? Or the camera that took them?" Lydia said. She wasn't sure if the police could match pictures with a camera, if some sort of information about the camera would be encoded with the photo.

"I have the camera," Holly said, pointing to the one sitting on the table. "But I gave Jennifer all the memory cards. And we have identical cameras, so I don't think you could trace them." She took another sip of coffee and ate a bit more of her cookie, falling into deep contemplation.

"Jennifer's gotten weird. *Weirder*, since Ricky died," Holly said slowly. "She's always been kind of crazy and wild. But now she's talking about miracles and her visions, how the Virgin Mary visits her in her dreams. She said that she's been given leeway, to follow the will of God, not the will of man." She shivered.

"I see," Lydia said. "Do you think Jennifer's dangerous?"

Holly gave a bitter laugh. "She's always been dangerous," she said. "More dangerous? Possibly."

"I know the detective in charge of the case," Lydia said after a few moments. "Would you like to talk with him?" Though she had no intention of introducing Holly to Detective Bloyer. Instead, she was planning on calling Ellis.

"But won't I go to jail? For being an accomplice?" Holly asked, sounding miserable.

"You didn't know what Jennifer was going to do, right?" Lydia said.

Holly shook her head vehemently. "I didn't. I really didn't."

"And she still hasn't said anything to you about it, right? You just have suspicions," Lydia said.

"True," Holly said. "What if they won't listen to me?"

"I'll make sure they do," Lydia promised her. "Since you didn't know about the murder, and you haven't helped her since then, but are coming forward with your suspicions, I don't think they can accuse you of being an accomplice after the fact."

Holly nodded. She broke her cookie and then started eating the crumbs, one by one. "I don't know. She's my sister."

"She's quite possibly a murderer," Lydia said. "I would want to know for certain. The police may find her innocent." She had serious doubts about that, but it was probably better for Holly to think that it was possible.

"All right," Holly said after a moment. "I'll do it. I'll talk with the police."

"Let me give them a call," Lydia said.

She called Ellis, glad that she hadn't removed his information from her phone.

Luckily, he answered right away.

"Detective Avery?" she asked, signaling to him that this was an official call.

"Yes, Ms. Marsh?" Ellis replied, obviously in cop mode.

Lydia quickly explained the situation. She could hear Ellis sigh but he didn't interrupt her.

"As Detective Bloyer is currently not in the office, I would be happy to take Holly's statement at this time," Ellis said. "However, it would be better if she were to come to Yakima to talk with an officer in person."

Lydia looked over at Holly, who seemed dazed by what she'd admitted to. "Hang on," Lydia said to Ellis.

"Road trip?" Lydia proposed to Holly. "To Yakima, to talk with the detectives there?"

Holly blinked, then nodded, giving her a real smile.

"Sure," she said. "I was thinking about getting away from here for a while anyway."

"We'll be there in about two hours," Lydia told Ellis.

"Thank you," Ellis told Lydia, sounding more friendly.

"See you soon," Lydia said.

When she swiped her phone off, Holly was giving her a big grin.

"Sounds like you and the detective have a thing going," she said. "Is he the guy you're going to marry?"

Lydia shook her head. "We just broke up," she said truthfully, not wanting to admit to Holly that she'd been lying about the wedding.

"That's awful!" Holly said. "Don't tell Jennifer. She might offer to help you get revenge."

"I won't," Lydia said. "Let's get ready for our road trip."

She had to call Misty to let her know. Maybe call her mom. Stay with Holly the entire time, though, so the other woman didn't get cold feet. Get her to Yakima, and maybe put Detective Bloyer in his place if he tried playing rough.

Finding the truth was more important than her conflicted feelings at this point.

19

Two days later, Lydia was surprised to see that Ellis was calling her. Was it about Holly or Jennifer? Or had he changed his mind about them? Was he actually going to call and beg for them to get back together?

He'd been coolly professional when she and Holly had shown up at the station. Holly had vacillated between tearful remorse for turning against her sister, and heartfelt relief that she might actually be free of Jennifer once and for all. Lydia had been a wreck, having to be so stoic while driving them there.

Detective Bloyer had been there as well, but he, too, had maintained a professional demeanor while interviewing Holly. Maybe he figured she'd already cried enough.

Lydia had waited in the coffee shop two blocks away from the police station while the detective carried out his interview. Ellis told her later that he'd "sat in" during the interview. He didn't say anything about Detective Bloyer, but Lydia could read between the lines well enough that to see Ellis was aware that his presence would rein in the other detective so he wouldn't get belligerent.

Then she'd driven Holly to a hotel while the detectives went out to interview Jennifer. Though Lydia had called Holly, she'd been taken straight to voice mail, and Holly had never called her back.

So that had been the last that Lydia had heard about the case. She had been keeping track in the newspapers, but she hadn't seen anything.

"Hi Lydia," Ellis said. He sounded friendly but professional. Not fully cop mode, but about halfway there.

"Good afternoon, Ellis," Lydia said.

Alice's eyes grew big. "Hi, Ellis!" she called loudly.

Lydia shook her head and walked out of the laundry room and back into her apartment so that she could have a modicum of privacy while she talked with him.

"I wanted to keep you updated on Jennifer Hollingsworth and the case," Ellis said.

Lydia blinked, surprised. "Thank you," she said. "I appreciate it."

"I wouldn't normally say anything, but the case is very close to closed at this point," Ellis said. "Jennifer appeared before a judge this morning and pled guilty to first degree murder."

"Really?" Lydia said. "She admitted to doing it?"

"She didn't at first," Ellis said. "She was adamant it hadn't been her. Then we told her how Holly had told us about being at that wedding and taking those pictures. So

Jennifer had no alibi. We told her that we were going to get her cell phone data, to tell us where she'd been. That was enough to convince her to confess to the murder." He paused, sighing. "She even brought us to her staging room, as she called it. She had made plans to murder a lot of other people. Including both her second husband and Patrice."

"Wow," Lydia said. She was going to have to make sure that Patrice took extra precautions if Jennifer was ever released.

"Your name was also on the board," Ellis added.

Lydia stood there, stunned. "Why on earth would she be thinking of killing me?"

"You weren't on the 'planned' list, outlined in red," Ellis told her. "You were merely on the pink one, the 'kill if necessary' list. She had visited the B&B, earlier. You are going to want to change all the locks on all the rooms. She had a master, and we still aren't sure where she got it from."

"Alice," Lydia said. "She lost her keys back at the start of August. It was the first time she'd ever lost her keys. Poor girl had been heartbroken, thinking we would no longer trust her."

"And why didn't you change the locks then?" Ellis inquired.

"Height of busy season," Lydia said smoothly. That, plus the expense. "I'll get it taken care of tomorrow, though." And she would. She should have done it sooner, though she didn't think that would have saved Ricky's life.

"Anyway, Jennifer has been formally charged. I believe

her attorney will try to make a case that Jennifer is insane. He might be able to get it to stick. Jennifer knew what she was doing, and also knew that it was wrong. She also claims that she was following a higher law."

"Let me know how that goes, all right?" Lydia said. She was also going to make sure that Misty knew, and would keep track of things in Yakima for them.

"I will," Ellis promised. He paused, then said, "It was good to see you the other day."

"It was nice to be able to call someone I knew on the police force," Lydia admitted. She still wasn't sure if it had been good to see Ellis or not. He'd been friendly, but still a cop the whole time.

"But…" Ellis sighed. "It also really brought home to me how far apart we've drifted."

"I know," Lydia said. She found herself in that too-familiar position, standing in the middle of her living room with her arms wrapped around herself. "It really is all for the best."

"The break-up? Yeah. But not necessarily how you'd think," Ellis said. "I've gone back into therapy. I think…I think we got together too soon after my divorce. I'm not able to split off my work life enough."

"I'm glad you're seeing your therapist again," Lydia said. She found she still cared about Ellis as a person.

But she didn't have a deep well of sadness flowing out of her as they said goodbye. Surface sadness, sure.

It really was better this way.

She walked back into the laundry room, finding Alice there with her arms stacked high with sheets and comforters.

"Ready to get back to work?" Alice said with a big grin.

"I am," Lydia said.

She was more than ready for things to get back to normal. Or a new normal, at any rate.

20

*L*ydia arranged for the people at Heart Vineyards to come out and do a wine tasting at the B&B the next Friday night. She felt it would help give them closure. She didn't know who would come out—if it would be Nancy, the woman who'd given the tour of the wine-making facilities or someone else.

She found herself quite pleased when it turned out to be the man who'd run the tasting room. He wore a black shirt that evening that highlighted his pale coloring along with the freckles sprinkled across his nose and cheeks. He had a rugged jawline, firm and masculine. His copper-colored hair flowed back in soft waves from a broad, intelligent forehead and bright blue eyes.

"Hi, Sean," Lydia said after he introduced himself. "Come with me and I'll show you the setup. I've cleared some space in the walk-in for your cases of wine."

"This is your place?" Sean said, not moving, looking around the restaurant area.

"It is," Lydia said proudly. Sure, it might need some

updating. But she really enjoyed her space, her teapots, how everything flowed together.

"Gosh, I might have to hire you to come and design our tasting room," Sean said. "It's a little out of date."

Lydia nodded but didn't say anything. It would be gauche of her to agree too vehemently.

Sean appreciated the built-in cutting board in the kitchen counter, the walk-in refrigerator, and the cooktop. "This looks like the perfect setup for the amount of customers you get."

"It is," Lydia said. It was surprising to meet someone who understood that "bigger" wasn't necessarily "better."

Lydia helped Sean bring the cases of wine in, then started setting up the cheese and crackers that people could serve themselves with. Instead of putting them out on a pretty platter, Lydia created individual servings and put each into one of the astonishingly large collection of teacups she'd acquired recently. It was a good compromise between letting people serve themselves while not touching what would be other people's food.

By seven o'clock, everything was all ready to go and people started arriving. Her mom showed up, which didn't surprise her, but she brought Jen McGowen with her, which did. The pair of them each took a glass of wine and a serving of cheese and crackers and sat at one of the back tables, their heads together, plotting.

It turned out that Jen was looking for something more to do, outside of working on the farm all the time. Lydia's dad had teased her for setting up the perfect match, though he wasn't yet ready to declare if it had come from heaven or hell.

Alan had stopped at least some of his nastier attacks on Lydia's family. Not because of some miraculous change of heart, or even a sudden case of conscience, but because Misty had managed to dig up that Alan's current wife had a daughter from her first marriage who was gay.

Unless Alan really wanted to alienate all of his own family, he had to stop with the slurs. Misty implied that someone had talked with Alan about leaking the news. He'd changed his tune quickly at that point.

Patrice came for a while. She'd taken a few days off after she'd found out that she'd been on Jennifer's "to kill" list, but now seemed cheery as ever. And as glamorous, wearing a very pretty gray silk blouse over a pair of denim shorts, boho chic.

Lydia stood next to Sean and sighed looking out at her best friend, who drew people to her like a light drew moths. She'd never be so effortlessly attractive.

Sean nudged her with an elbow. "Aye, she's pretty, all right. But she doesn't have your head on her shoulders."

Lydia looked at him, puzzled.

Sean continued. "I remember now, that it was you I ran into after I stumbled across the body." For a moment, Sean seemed to go slightly paler, as if the memory still haunted him. "You didn't seem to be shaken at all. You got everything organized, getting everyone off the bus and back into the tasting room, got them all settled and kept them calm."

"Patrice would have done the same," Lydia declared. Probably. Patrice could be just as practical as Lydia in a pinch, though that wasn't her default mode.

"Maybe. Maybe not. But you were the one who was

there, who got us through it," Sean said. "I'm here to say thank you, as much as anything else."

"You're welcome," Lydia said. "I'm just glad that it's over." And she was. She and Ellis were really, truly, officially done. She'd had all the locks in the entire building re-keyed, including the lock on the lockbox in the laundry room. Though it would be a while before Jennifer's actual trial, she felt certain that justice would be served.

"What, you won't have us back?" Sean said in mock horror.

"I may, I may not," Lydia said. "That will depend on how the rest of the evening goes," she added, teasing.

Sean gave her broad wink. "I have my hopes."

Lydia just rolled her eyes at him before going back out into the crowd, picking up used teacups and wine glasses. She felt Sean's eyes on her as she worked.

He certainly was her type. He was local, and he shared her interest in providing for guests.

She gave him a smile before she walked back into the kitchen.

Maybe, when she was ready, he would be too.

In the meanwhile, she got to see to her guests and provide service from the heart.

ABOUT THE AUTHOR

Leah Cutter writes page-turning fiction in exotic locations, such as a magical New Orleans, the ancient Orient, Hungary, the Oregon coast, rural Kentucky, Seattle, Minneapolis, and many others.

She writes literary, fantasy, mystery, science fiction, and horror fiction. Her short fiction has been published in magazines like *Alfred Hitchcock's Mystery Magazine* and *Talebones*, anthologies like Fiction River, and on the web. Her long fiction has been published both by New York publishers as well as small presses.

Find Leah's books on Knotted Road Press at (www.KnottedRoadPress.com)

Follow her blog at www.LeahCutter.com.

Reviews

It's true. Reviews help me sell more books. If you've enjoyed this story, please consider leaving a review of it on your favorite site.

Come someplace new...

Are you a traveler? Do you enjoy exploring strange new worlds, new cultures, new people?

Journey into the various lands envisioned by Leah Cutter.

Sign up for my newsletter and I'll start you on your travels with a free copy of my book, *The Island Sampler*.

I will never spam you or use your email for nefarious purposes. You can also unsubscribe at any time.

http://www.LeahCutter.com/newsletter/

ABOUT KNOTTED ROAD PRESS

Knotted Road Press fiction specializes in dynamic writing set in mysterious, exotic locations.

Knotted Road Press non-fiction publishes autobiographies, business books, cookbooks, and how-to books with unique voices.

Knotted Road Press creates DRM-free ebooks as well as high-quality print books for readers around the world.

With authors in a variety of genres including literary, poetry, mystery, fantasy, and science fiction, Knotted Road Press has something for everyone.

Knotted Road Press
www.KnottedRoadPress.com